FROM BIRTHING WATERS

From Birthing Waters

NTERANYA SANGINGA

Vert Publishing

Illustrations by Jamal Fleurby "Creator" Mabulay

Published by Vert Publishing

First Publication Date: 25 April 2024

ISBN: 978-0-646-89455-3

For permission requests, write to the publisher, addressed "Attention: Permissions Coordinator," at the address below.
Vert Publishing
Silver Stream Estate
Silver Lakes
Pretoria
South Africa
info@vertcorp.co.za

The characters and events portrayed in this book are fictitious. Any similarity to real persons, living or dead, is coincidental and not intended by the author.

CONTENTS

v

"Uta onea ku batoto yako"

Tate Ernestine Balemba Buhendwa / Ma Konda

~ One ~

SWEET PLANTAIN

If he leaves, she will no longer need me. What will I do then?

Brian had two suitcases. One was filled with clothes, shoes, and small things he carried, like the letter I wrote him 10 years ago when I first learned to write. It was not a long letter, just a simple one that most children write at that age, but he kept it in between the pages of his journal.

When I asked, *"Kaka, you still keep this letter?"*

"Of course! I need to remember when you were small and cute before you became someone too cool for me."

"Ahhh, me? Never! Let me write you a new one; you can't show your future wife that one. I have better handwriting now; don't be going and embarrassing me."

"Are you saying you are embarrassed by me?"

"You have started. Today, I won't play your games."

"Is that so? You're a big girl now, henh? Sawa! We will see."

I never wrote a new one because, deep down, I knew it wasn't the same thing. It would be forced. The child who wrote that wrote it genuinely, and it would do Brian good to remember that, even when I didn't talk to him, which would be more frequent now.

In his other suitcase, he put some clothes, a heavy jacket, and a blanket for the cold. Mama had also cooked food and put it in containers that she then wrapped in newspapers and sellotaped so much that three rolls were finished by the end. She had said,

"If those soldiers at the border want to open your bag and look in it, they will need first to sit down and swear small. Busy, busy intimidating people and throwing their things! Then, they will still ask you for some money with their big bellies - even a pregnant woman... Eish! No shame at all."

How Mama spoke, people would think she crossed borders often, but getting her in a taxi these days was impossible. At least today, Brian, her baby, had convinced her to come with him in the taxi to the airport; even the angels will dance today because Brian is going. It might have also been the prayers that Mama Kangele and Mama did over the phone at 5 AM. Mama had whispered through the prayer, trying not to wake the rest of us as she prayed with her sister, Mama Kangele. Even though Mama Kangele had been with us until 1 AM, she and Mama had spent the past week going to town every day. She would remind Mama that Brian would need shoes, and they would run to the market to get as many shoes as possible. Then, when they would return, she would remember that he needed a good heavy jacket like the one her brother wore in the picture he sent her; we all used to see it on the wall shelf in her sitting room.

It was only Mama Kangele who was able to convince Mama to step outside of the house. She would show her where to buy the best fruits and meat in the market. Mama even took me with them once to learn how to buy meat. Mama Kangele was the best at knowing where to go to get good tailors. Many tailors could sow, but very few could make a dress by the day it was wanted, and she knew them all. She and Mama always looked so beautiful at weddings that they started being put at tables in the back.

When Mama had gotten upset by this, Mama Kangele said, "*Da José, you are worried about a jealous woman. They are trying to keep their husbands, who like to run to other women. But are you a woman who will know another woman's husband, Da José? Of course not! So, you have nothing to worry about. Let them be jealous.*"

Mama did not stop going to weddings with Mama Kangele after that. Brian may have softened her resistance to him leaving and taking him to the airport, but it had to be Mama Kangele who convinced her when they prayed over the phone.

As the two continued to talk, Mama started to reach for his hair. I left them and went outside, where I had left a pot of potatoes with carrots and peas to cook over charcoal slowly. Mbabula, or stoovu, as we heard the Ugandan say when he found Mama cooking. Mukasa had come here with an NGO giving injections to women to protect them from some disease, but Mama was too old, and I was too young. He said he would come back in three years. But Brian would be back for me before then - at least, that's what he promised me.

*****

"*Mwana wangu, won't you cut this hair? How long has it been since you even saw a salon?*"

"*Mama, not this again,*" Brian replied, trying to keep his tone light.

"*Ah ah, Brian! You know I don't want you going there and people saying you are dirty? You know your mother likes us to be known as clean people, eh my son.*"

"*Mama, I will make sure to wash them and oil them.*"

"*But what if you don't have time? You know how you used to spend all your time in that cybercafe? Will you really have time? Now, if you cut your hair, then you would not even need to wash and oil.*"

"*Yes, Mama, but where I am going, it will cost me more than 20,000 francs to cut my hair. Now, with this head of mine like Baba, you know that my hair will already be back in two or three days after cutting.*"

"*Hehehe, yes, your father gave you that Samson head.*"

I was about to tell her that's why she loved me so much when Bené walked in. She carried a plate steaming with freshly boiled carrots mixed with small yellow potatoes.

"*You better be the one eating that food.*"

"*This one is for you; mine is the rest of the pot since you are travel-ling,*" Bené replied, handing him a plate.

"*I can't eat right now,*" Brian admitted, looking at the food but not touching it.

"*Why? Is it because you are going over there that you can no longer eat your sister's food?*" Mama asked.

"*Tell him, Mama! He is now a big man. See him!*"

"*Me, I don't like this two against one.*"

"*What two against one? You are the one against yourself refusing to eat. I could have saved the charcoal.*"

"*Bené, if I eat now, I will be gassing for the officer when they ask for my passport. And don't worry, Papa Innocent said they will give me food when I am on the plane.*"

"*You're lucky you are older than me, or I would have sat you right here and fed you,*" Bené said as she patted her lap to show she was not joking. My stomach was not at ease, and eating something now would be like the National exam. Back then, I was so focused on beating Francois in the exams that the stress of wanting to be first in class made me vomit for breakfast, lunch, and dinner.

"*Brian, before we go, call Ma Mukubwa,*" Mama said, handing me her Nokia to call Mama Kangele.

"*Jambo Mama Kangele, it's me Brian.*"

"*Mutoto wangu! I am so happy to hear your voice. Are you ready to go?*"

"*Yes Mama. I am ready.*"

"*That is good, very good. I am sure Da José has already made you pray,*" she said calmly. "*I spoke with her this morning to tell her to tell you sorry. Shanga José fell sick last night, and I have been at Generale with her since then.*"

"*Yes, Mama told me this morning. I hope Shanga gets better.*"

"*I really wanted to take you to the airport, but it was not God's plan. But you go well and make us proud. I have prayed for you, and I am sure you will do well. God is protecting you.*"

"*Amen. Thank you very much, Mama.*"

"*And when you become a big man over there, and we see you on the television on TV5 or France24, remember us too.*"

"*Of course, Mama! I can never forget you. Mama, Bené and you will be joining me when I get money. I will take care of all of you.*"

"*Amen. Amen. I will be waiting for my big car.*"

"*Yes, Mama and you will never have to pay for a taxi ever again.*"

"*You will go far, Brian. God Bless you.*"

"*Thank you, Mama! And thank you for the fifty dollars you gave Mama to give me.*"

"*You are very welcome, Brian. That is to help you with your books and to buy small spaghetti.*"

"*Thank you, Mama. Mama, I have to go. Papa Jacques is here.*"

"*Okay, my son. Go well and be careful there. Don't forget who you are, and don't forget us.*"

"*I will not, Mama. Please take care of Mama and Bené for me.*"

"*Of course. Bye, my son.*"

"*Sawa, Da Ngele! Let me escort our son to the airport,*" Mama said as she took her Nokia from me and cut the phone.

Papa Jacques hooted three times; he was early. We had agreed he would come at 11 with his big Noah taxi, but here he was at 10:30 a.m. I removed the hair bands from my locs and fluffed them out. Three years, and what had started as an experiment lay on my shoulder blades at full length and got me many "Rastafari" greetings.

"*Bené, I have left some clothes in the Osuofia bag. Just because I am not here does not mean you can wear them.*"

"*But what happens if some fall out? You know, wearing clothes keeps them fresh so the rats in your room won't eat them. But if you want to have clothes with holes like Nana, who walks with her lolos showing.*"

"*Bené! Stop talking nonsense and help your brother carry one of these bags to Papa Jacques.*"

Bené kept quiet, but she looked at me, and I could see that she was laughing on the inside. I gave her the smaller black bag with more of my clothes and shoes and the oils for my hair. I opened our green metal door as Mama closed the curtains that were as old as Bené.

"Jambo Papa Jacques, habari ya Mama Jacques na Jacques?" Bené greeted Papa Jacques as she always did, asking about Mama Jacques and Jacques. But her real interest was in how Jacques was doing.

"Wako sawa kabisa!" Papa Jacques laughed, and the gap between the buttons of his crisscrossed blue and white shirt widened when his stomach pushed out. He liked Bené and saw her as a daughter, someone Jacques could one day marry. If only Jacques knew what these two both wanted.

"Asante Papa Jacques, for driving us to the airport. I know una customers wengi, so I am really grateful."

"Ah, Brayo! This is nothing. When you become Mheshimwa, just remember me, si ndio?" We laughed and shook hands, but we both knew he was serious. This ride was free today with the hopes that if I became someone important, his family would also be taken care of. I helped Papa Jacques put both suitcases in the back of the taxi.

"Baba Jacques! Asante sana! Mungu akubariki na akurudishie!"

"Ah Mama Brayo, si uko ndugu!" Papa Jacques was quick to receive the thanks. I wondered whether he had gotten tired of

receiving praise that ended with long, long prayers about great-grandchildren he would never see. We entered the car with me at the front with Papa Jacques, and Bené sat with Mama behind us. The drive would take 45 minutes if there was no traffic, no accidents, and no driver thinking they could fit their car on the boundary line between two vehicles.

Since it was going to be a long drive, I asked Papa Jacques about how it was growing up before the day the General shot the Governor. With older men, politics always worked. With mothers, it was about the most recent newlyweds in town and how young people are making bad choices. If I asked a question, I added, "Ahhhh." "Ohhhh" and "Hmm" at the end of everything they said, they would keep going without too much needed from me.

Papa Jacques told us about how the morning before the governor was killed, he and his friends were playing football, and his team was winning 2 to 1. They were about to score another goal when they saw military cars driving by at full speed, and all at once, the mothers selling their food in the markets grabbed whatever they could along with their children. Everyone began to run in different directions, and he did, too. He and his brother ran so fast that they found themselves at the bottom of the hill by the fishermen's nets and boats. They jumped into one, lay flat and covered themselves with the net. When the night came, and things were silent, they climbed up the hill back to where they had been playing football. There, they found a body flattened on the ground. At first, they didn't recognise the figure until they saw the cowrie shell anklet. It was Papa Jacques' classmate, Alain, whose cowrie shell anklet had been given to him by his late grandfather as a gift.

"You see, the thing about change, Brayo, is that when it comes, you have to be fast, but you also have to be careful. Yes, it was his time, but if he had not been careless, he would have heard and seen the truck, and he would still be alive today."

It was a bitter thing to say, but most elders who were there that day and the days after had never let go of the bitterness. At least he talked about it; Mama would have just changed the subject. Papa Jacques continued telling us how he and his brother carried their other sisters and brothers across the river and then over the border. He saw mosquitoes swollen with all the blood they took from the many running away. Even his mother had a fever for three weeks, and it was only through prayer that she was able to stand up again.

"See, Brayo, you children of today have it easier than us, your parents. That is why you must remain focused on where you are going. Don't let people put you in things that will not be good for you."

Papa Jacques quickly shifted the gear into first as he slowed down to a stop and parked. Forty-five minutes had flown by with his stories, and we both hopped out to get the suitcases from the back of his silver Noah. Bené, after setting Mama aside, pushed a trolley right between Papa Jacques and me to load the two suitcases.

"Sawa Brayo! This is not goodbye. Travel safely and make us proud!"

Papa Jacques shook my hand and pulled me in for a big embrace like a father would a son. He let go and closed the back of the Noah, then hopped into the driver's seat. He was not going to leave just yet, but he also knew that as close as we were, blood was closer.

"Okay, Bené, remember what we agreed. You study well and take care of Mama. I don't want to hear that you have disturbed her blood pressure, okay?"

"Who are you telling to take care of who? This one! Ha! It's as if you don't know your sister." Mama jumped in, but even though she looked serious, I had come to know that these two enjoyed their cat-and-mouse game.

"I will try to call you on Bené's WhatsApp when I reach you, but it might be very late. It will be okay." I held both their hands in one hand and could see Bené holding back her tears and the folds on Mama's forehead when unsure about something.

"What can I do? If I cannot get you to cut your hair, how can I stop this? Go well, and remember you are my son; do not bring me shame, I beg you." As she spoke, Mama came in and hugged me tightly. Bené stood still, holding my hand but looking away. I pulled her in, too, and held both my women tight. Mama rubbed and patted my back as if soothing a child, but in truth, she was soothing her own heart.

When we finally let go, Mama brought the wrapper to her face, wiping away the tears and mucus that had managed to escape her for the first time since Baba.

"If you forget me, I will come and find you myself and beat you," Bené said, punching me in the shoulder.

"*I love you too.*" I grabbed my black bag with my charger, passport and other documents from her shoulder and walked towards the airport entrance. The police at the front began their usual conversation, asking about information they didn't need to know. But if one didn't know how to answer, they would have to part with the highest currency note in their wallet. For me, that was the $20 Papa Jacques had slipped into my hand during our handshake. I stuck to a script of being a student and having no money but promising that I would not forget them when I came back home when I graduated. Eventually, they let me pass.

A woman then pointed towards a line leading to four metal boxes with people sitting behind them. Each one had a table on which people were putting their suitcases, and then the suitcases were rolled away into a hole in the wall. Mama Juliet had told me that my suitcases had to be less than 23 kilograms, but to be safe, I should not exceed 21 kilograms because the airport always adds one kilogram to your suitcase so that they can try to get more people to pay more.

When my turn came, I prepared my smile and the sentences I had been practising. Mama had said to make sure that I only talked to women. She said that men do not understand each other, and women do the same. But if a woman deals with a man, the man will be kind to her. And if a man is dealing with a woman, the woman will be more forgiving.

"*Good afternoon. How are you today?*"

"*Passport!*"

"*Yes, here it is, and my ticket is as well.*"

"Put your first suitcase here," she said, pointing to the table. I placed the heavier one on it first.

"I am travelling for school. I will attend university to complete a Bachelor's in computer science."

"22.8 kilograms. Next suitcase!" That was close. I lifted the second one onto the table.

"20 kilograms. Here are your boarding passes. You follow those people upstairs, and your boarding gate will be A5."

"Thank you very much, madam." I smiled and grabbed my passport and the thing she printed before she could change her mind. I didn't ask what she meant by boarding pass or boarding gate but followed the other people on their way up the stairs.

I only took two steps up the stairs when I felt a hand on my shoulder. I looked back to see the policeman I had met at the entrance.

"Are you Brian?"

"Yes, how did you know?"

"Your mother asked me to look for a boy with dreadlocks like Bob Marley. She says she has to see you and tell you something."
*****

One day, someone in this neighbourhood will shoot Susu for barking for the whole village. I reached for my phone. 10 messages and two missed calls. Jacques had messaged me asking about whether I was ready for the exam. This boy! What was interesting about exams? Brian had called twice at 3 AM. Very late, like he had said, but he left a voice note instead of calling a third time. A long one. Five minutes long. I played the voice note, but nothing came out. I looked for earphones under my pillow and plugged them in, but there was still nothing. I pulled on the wire to see if that was the issue. Sometimes, pulling on the cable made them work after Nancy stepped on them while playing Kange. There was nothing in the voice note but some mumbling like an engine. Brian had promised to send me a new phone when he had enough money.

"*Mama! Mama! Mama!*"

"*Ahhh what is it Bené?*" Mama responded from outside, where she was peeling onions.

"*Brian has reached.*"

"*Did you talk to him?*"

"*No, but he called me twice when we were sleeping.*"

"*We thank God,*" Mama said as she lifted her hands from the tray of onions and began to sing, her eyes closed and face lifted towards the sky. She would move from side to side, rocking the stool slightly, yet always finding balance as she continued to sing. I put on a dera and wrapped a wrapper around my chest, preparing to help Mama with the onions. Walking outside in just a dera would have been unacceptable; she would have chased me back inside for showing my breasts— a behaviour reserved for older women who had borne many children. In our community, young women who showed their breasts would never be married.

I dragged the other stool from the stoovu to sit right opposite Mama. She already had a tray beside her. Whether it was for her or she had planned to put me to work, I didn't know. I pulled some onions from the basket on the ground and put them on my tray. We sang songs as we worked: Mama led one, and I another. We cleared our trays of onion skin and started cutting each onion into smaller pieces. I was beginning to sing "Hakuna Mungu Kama wewe" when we heard banging and hooting at our door. Mama jumped from her stool.

"Mama, calm down now. Are you the governor?"

"Bené! What have I told you about saying such things?"

"It's okay, Mama. Let me see who it is. I will be careful." I walked slowly towards the green metal gate, avoiding the stones and sand. When we were younger, Baba had taken a knife and cut a slit into the gate at an angle so only we could see anyone at our door.

It was Papa Jacques with a short man in a suit and tie that I had never seen in my life. He had no hair on his face except for his eyebrows and kept wiping away the sweat with his handkerchief. Brian had said men like this never went anywhere without an Air conditioner. Their offices were colder than fridges, they slept with an air conditioner, and even their cars had one. I didn't know him, but Papa Jacques would never bring anyone to our door without being sure first.

Without opening the door, I said, *"Jambo Papa Jacques. I hope nothing is wrong."*

"Bené, is your mother home?" Papa Jacques responded without his usual tone. He knew Mama would be in. Mama never went anywhere after 9 a.m. except for church, a wedding, or a funeral.

"Yes, she is."

"Please go and get her."

"Mama! Papa Jacques is here to see you!" I called from the door, but she was already coming outside to see what had taken me so long. I opened the gate, and Papa Jacques entered, followed by the man.

"Hello Madam, my name is Francis Rwabagire and I work at the airport. Are you Brian Mudjozi's mother?" The sweaty man asked. Did he come to tell us that Brian had reached safely? We already knew that. Mama did not respond straight away.

"Yes."

"Madam, I do not know how to tell you this, but we were informed early this morning that Brian did not make it." As the sweaty man finished his sentence, Mama's body fell to the ground, and she just sat there. She did not say a word, did not look at anyone, and just rubbed her thighs.

"*Giselle! Giselle! Giselle, stand up! You have to stand up.*" Papa Jacques began to lift Mama by her armpits. Mama did not move.

"*Bené! Go and call Ngele! Bené! NOW!*" I jumped at Papa Jacques, raising his voice, and ran out the door. I didn't stop until I got to Mama Kangele. Somewhere between Papa Jacques shouting and reaching Mama Kangele's house, I started crying. Mama Kangele opened the door for me.

When she saw my tears, she asked, "*Bené mutoto wangu ni nini? Why are you crying?*"

"*Mama, Mama won't stand up!*"

"*What do you mean she won't stand up? Did she fall?*"

"*No.*" I was trying to speak, but I couldn't breathe. "*Some man in a suit from the airport came to our house. He said Brian didn't make it.*"

"*Yesu!*" Mama Kangele dropped her bag and pulled off her headscarf. She grabbed my hand, and we ran back to the house. When we arrived, Papa Jacques was in the car with Mama and the sweaty man.

"*Da José! Da José! Yesu! Da José! Hapana! Mutoto wetu wehhhh!*" Mama Kangele entered the car and started holding Mama. I squeezed myself beside her. Brian had called me. He said he was going to call me when he got there safely. Mama Kangele's corn-rows rubbed against me as she rocked Mama. Mama did not cry. She did not speak. She did not move. The radio played Kidum's Mapenzi, Nameless' Sinzia, and Jaguar's Kigeugeu. Brian used to know these songs by heart, even the dance for each part. When Mama was sleeping, he taught me. I don't remember what else played, but the sweaty man handed me his napkin when the car stopped. We were back at the airport.

We passed by a policeman who greeted us and led us through the airport entrance, down a hallway with flickering lights and yellow paint coming off the walls, and into a very cold room with a table in the middle. On it was something with a white blanket. The sweaty man pulled the white blanket aside, and Mama howled—a howl that came from deep within and turned into screams as she ran to the table.

"*Mutoto wangu lamuka baba! Brian lamuka! Usini ache ivi mutoto wangu.*" The policeman left the room as Mama held onto Brian's body. Papa Jacques looked up, crossing his arms. Men do not cry, but even this was hard for Papa Jacques.

"*Usinache mutoto wangu! Brian weh! Lamuka! Bené, help me. Help me wake your brother.*" I froze, but Mama Kangele stood behind Mama, holding her up as her knees collapsed. Mama wiped the locs away from Brian's face and placed his head on her chest, hugging him tight as if the tighter she held him, Brian would wake up and tell us it was all a joke.

The policeman came back in with papers and explained that there were forms that had to be signed for Brian's body. Mama Kangele and Papa Jacques spoke slowly to Mama, peeling her hands off Brian. Brian, you promised me. You promised me. Mama signed the forms, and Papa Jacques spoke to the sweaty man and the policeman about the costs. He gave them his number and told them he would cover the fees. The sweaty man shook his hand and then mine. The policeman did the same, but when he reached me, he stopped.

"*Are you his sister?*" I nodded but kept my eyes on Brian.

"*I am sorry. I can only imagine what you are going through, but you must be strong. Be strong for your mother. I can see you are a strong girl. You will get through this if you stay close to your mother. She needs you the most right now.*"

He pressed my shoulder and then said, "*Promise?*"

He reached out with his hand to shake mine, and we shook hands quickly before he walked out.

When we got home that evening, Mama Kangele fed Mama and watched over her. I opened the gate for Papa Jacques, who brought fruits, water bottles, and a mattress. Tomorrow, people would visit us to tell us about Brian and cry for us. People who wanted to see Mama and then tell people that her son had died because she had killed her husband. They would still eat the fruits and drink all there was to drink. Mama and I would have to sit on the mattress for everyone who passed. After arranging the room, I returned to my bed and Brian's voice note. What had he tried to tell me? Was he calling me to say to me that something was wrong? Did he know?

I reached into my pocket and unfolded the piece of paper that the policeman had given me. It read:

0995 978 324. Message me when you are alone. There is something you and your Mum do not know.

*****

"*Da Ngele. We are sisters, not so?*" Mama whispered from the blue plastic chair she sat in. Her voice just reached beyond the bars.

"*José, how can you ask me that in front of Bené?*" I looked straight at her in the blue dress, her cornrows undone and ropes tied around her brown wrists with black knuckles.

Mama remained still and asked again softly, "*Da Ngele. We are sisters, not so?*"

Mama waited for Mama Kangele to respond, but she did not look at Mama and kept quiet.

"*Da Ngele, why? What did I do to you? Me, who has never said anything bad about you. Me, who, when you were sick, I left my husband with a three-month-old Bené to take care of you. Da Ngele, I pray God!*" Mama stopped. Even now, after all that had happened, Mama Kangele was still her Da Ngele.

"*Bené, come and help me.*" Mama had sunk into the blue plastic chair like a three-year-old child. She held onto my hand with one hand and wrapper with the other as I pulled her up to stand. We left Mama Kangele, Mama did not turn and neither did I. Papa Jacques drove us home chewing on a toothpick as the radio played. No one said anything. There was nothing to say.

*****

"Bené! What were you about to do?"

"Nothing." But I smiled, and my eyes darted from Brian to the ground.

"Is that money you were about to pick off the ground?"

"Ahhh, it's 20 dollars Kaka! Come on!"

"Go ahead and pick it then. You will make good goat stew, or maybe Mama will grind you into cassava flour."

"This is not Nigeria, abego!" I retorted, but I left the money. In this neighbourhood, anything with four legs had a short life span.

"You're lucky it's not raining! Let's go home and tell Mama the news." Brian smiled. I could see him exhale after all his hours in the cyber cafe next to Jojo's shop. He had done it. Brian was going to America, where Michelle Obama, Missy Elliot and Madea lived. Even though I would not see Jojo as often anymore, it was going to be great!

Jojo's TV in the corner of his poster-filled wooden kiosk taught us that in Nigeria, you never pick money off the ground. It also taught us that in Cote d'Ivoire, some women carried snakes in their woman parts, and they would bite rich men so that they died poor. This was when Jojo did not have any new Jet Li, Jackie Chan, Jason Stratham, or Angelina Jolie movies.

When there was no power, Jojo turned on his radio, and there we learnt of a story of a man in South Africa who had angered his in-laws by treating his wife so badly that on a sunny day, he was struck by lightning. The same channel warned of thieves who used magic to control and rob you in Kenya.

These thieves had mastered the magic of hypnosis. They carried one ever so gently from the touch of a street child to the teller at Equity Bank. When the money was securely within their different bags, next to the jewellery taken from the house, their target was returned to their home. Their memory of the event was formatted like an SD card. Clean, efficient, and almost harmless. The more robbers robbed, the less street children received ears to listen, hearts to pity, and open pockets to give.

*****

When the policeman called me that evening, he asked if none of the Mamas were near me. He then said that he was there the day that Brian was travelling, and he remembered him because he had Bob Marley hair but was very polite, unlike other boys with the same hair. I kept quiet, trying to understand why this policeman who did not know Brian was now grieving him on the phone with me.

"Did Brian eat anything that morning? Did you cook anything for him?"

"I made potatoes, but Brian refused to eat anything."

"So it has to be her."

"Who?"

A woman approached him at the entrance, begging that she had forgotten to give her son his food for his travels. He said the woman told him he had gotten a scholarship and was going to America to study at a big university. He said the woman pleaded and started crying, that he felt bad for her and thought of his mother. He brought Brian outside and saw Brian hug the woman who said she was his mother. She then gave him a glass bowl of plantain. Brian's favourite.

The policeman was sure it was plantain because he checked the glass bowl when Brian entered. The airport staff had been talking to each other when they heard the news, and the policeman had heard one of them say Brian had refused to eat anything on the plane.

"*Do you remember the woman?*"

"*Yes, she was with you when you came to see the body.*"

"*The one who was screaming and holding the body?*"

"*No, the other one with the hair.*"

They are all thieves. Some rob money, some rob minds and some rob souls. She robbed us of lives we prayed for, begged for and toiled for. She robbed Mama - but she had done so from the start. She robbed Brian of all the dreams he was to breathe. She robbed me, not just of my brother, but of memories and trust. How does one swallow, knowing that their mother killed their brother?

Plantains are bitter now.

"*Bené,*" Mama called out.

"*Yes, Mama?*"

"*It's okay.*"

~ Two ~

KNOCKING ON WOOD

Another child might be born today. No, not mine, not hers, and not of someone we know. At least, I think I don't know them. But I know that someone somewhere may be carrying a seed.

Do they want it? Did they want it in the first place? I wonder, when a bird shits, does it ask the soil if the seed it swallowed can find a home in its womb. And if they didn't want the child? Why? It is a life that had yet to be lived and witnessed in this form. Children are a gift, but even the most priceless gifts have a cost. Can it be paid? Or is the child destined to visit a womb and return without breathing the fire that exists outside the labia?

These days, a white plastic stick tells people that they are with child. One fills their bladder and then releases it into the stick. Then, in less than 10 minutes, one or two lines appear. There is little room for error, intuition, and lies. This was different from the days of Mama Lolo.

She lived above us in the apartment Baba had built with money from selling some of the land Gogo Anna left him to a business. Baba had made it three bedrooms; if he had had more money, he would have built four rooms. More space for people who would come for his children's weddings. Until then, he would make money with it by housing Mama Lolo and her husband, Papa Christian.

Papa Christian wore a silver metal watch that was too big for his wrist. It wasn't odd because many uncles who came by did the same. Someone somewhere had told them that watches that were big for the wrist showed signs of wealth or wealth to come. As for Papa Christian, he always spoke of how the business he was doing was going to bring him so much money he would hire all of us children. What was odd, was that he wore the watch on his right hand.

When they first moved in, Papa Christian would stop by Baba's every evening to listen to the radio with him and talk politics. Every other week, he would find a different way of trying to ask Baba about what his plans for the house were. Baba would smile every time and pretend to think about it for some time before telling him that he was still unsure about it. We would laugh on some evenings about it with Baba, as he would tell us that Papa Christian wanted his house and thought that he would give it to him. But Baba would act as if he was not giving it too much thought to avoid any discussions of a payment plan. A payment plan to Baba was a trap. Papa Christian would begin to pay, and along the way, he would start to have issues, and by then, it would be too late to get him out of the house.

When they first moved in, it was just the three of them: Mama Lolo, Papa Christian, and their son Lucien. Mama Lolo often joined my mother to prepare food for their husbands, sharing laughter and reminiscing about their secondary school days. They would also try to recall the different girls they had grown up with, discussing where they were now and who they had married. This had continued, until one day when Papa Christian came back home early—no food on the table waiting for him, and Mama Lolo was nowhere to be found in the house. He marched downstairs shouting for his wife, Louise. His shouts for his wife echoed so loudly that the entire neighbourhood thought Mama Lolo was in trouble.

Caught off guard and barely grasping what was happening, Mama Lolo didn't hear her husband's calls until he had already grabbed her hand. Clutching her wrapper to prevent it from slipping off her waist, she was pulled up the stairs and into their apartment by a furious Papa Christian.

We all heard Papa Christian shouting, but Mama sent us back to playing and threatened that she would make it painful to sit if we stopped. So, I pulled Lucien back into the game. After about thirty minutes, Papa Christian went silent, and Mama called us back into the house to eat. Baba's radio was louder than usual on the wooden bench.

More than an hour had passed since Papa Christian came and took Mama Lolo away. We finished eating and prepared the table for our homework with a candle and kerosene lamp in the middle. By the time I wrapped up my biology studies and Lucien began tackling his additional mathematics, the power would be out, as it always was by that hour.

Mama Lolo returned after three hours wearing a red dress, red shoes and a lot of red lipstick. We could see it even when she was not near the candle. She apologised to Mama for Papa Christian's earlier behaviour and explained that she had forgotten about a special dinner they had been invited to and were extremely late for. Papa Christian had slept after the dinner from fatigue from work, but he never mentioned it to Baba the next day and Baba never asked.

Later that week, Mama sat me down and asked me if Lucien had been behaving differently. Lucien was a bit quieter than usual, but it was exam time, and he was always quieter when there was a lot of work. Mama sighed as if my response was not what she was looking for. From that day with her, Lucien began to spend more and more time with us. We learned to share the bed so we could both get enough sleep. The bed was not really the problem, but the sharing of the blanket. He was still better than Francine, who, at two years old, kicked me in the mouth in the middle of the night.

That same year, Mama Lolo informed Mama that Lucien would soon become a kaka like me, his brother. Even though I was Lucien's younger brother, he would get his very own Francine. Every day from then, Lucien and I would meet Papa Christian after school at the gate to our homes. He would sit at the corner listening to the radio on the wooden bench and set up Muchuba for when Baba arrived. If Mama or Mama Lolo dropped a pot or the mwiko was stirred forcefully, Papa Christian would run into the kitchen to make sure his wife and child were fine. Lucien and I started dropping pans just so we could laugh when he came running. The very first time we did it, he warned Mama that she should make sure nothing happened to Mama Lolo or they would have a problem.

Mama did not respond to Papa Christian, but she stopped Mama Lolo from doing much of the work. If she saw her crouch, we would be called to witness how she wanted to cause trouble for Mama. When Mama would settle, she'd ask her to sing, and they would sing Yahwe Kumama and Nakushukura. If we didn't also join, then Lucien and I would be called stubborn children who refuse to pray. So even as we worked on the homework that our teacher, Ingenieur Nzolantima Nzabonimpa, gave us, we would add our squeaky "Kumama" and "eh bwana". After praising the Lord, they would go into songs from when they were girls until one of them would remember a story about a song they were singing. It was about how the choir leader with the most beautiful voice had the meanest spirit in the dorms or the one girl who thought she could sing and embarrassed herself in front of the principal and the entire school.

When it got hard for Mama Lolo to walk up the stairs, Papa Christian would let her lean on him and wait through the twenty minutes. Until one day, he came running down at 2 a.m. calling for Mama. Lucien and I were woken up by Mama knocking on our door as she tried to tie her wrapper and wear the slippers that Ma Mudogo had brought for her from Kenya. As she walked out the door, she gave Lucien and I orders. We were to serve Papa Christian and Baba the beers that were at the bottom of the fridge. She always kept four beers at the bottom of the fridge in case Baba surprised her with guests. They always were on the bottom shelf because if they cracked from the cold, the rest of the food would not smell or taste like bad beer. Lucien was to put the meat with sauce in a pot and add a bit of water to warm it up over one mbabula, as I made bugali. Mama had taught me to smell when the flour began to stick to the pot before it burnt for Baba. I made Baba's hard bugali when Mama joined the other mamas for evening vigils. Baba came into the sitting room to meet Papa Christian with a Kanga wrapped around his waist and white vest. Papa Christian was walking back and forth in chequered blue shorts and a worn-out Washington DC t-shirt.

Baba sent us back to our room once we had served them their beers and the food. Even with everything that was happening, he expected us to wake up for school when Chikudu croaked and Pululu bleated. When Lucien and I woke up the next morning, Mama met us with songs of grace to the Almighty. Mama Lolo had given birth to a girl whom Papa Christian named Christelle. This was only after Mama had cleaned and wrapped Mama Lolo. She told us that men were never to look or see a woman in such a position, or they were bound to go mad from the shock. She sent us off to school, but the moment it was over, Lucien ran the entire way back home. When I finally got home, I saw him through the window, sitting with a lot of white blankets on his lap. Mama Lolo sat beside him, so close that a toothpick could not fit between them. Papa Christian joined them, carrying a glass that he then handed to Mama Lolo before taking Christelle from Lucien. As much as I wanted to see Christelle, I knew that Mama and Baba were probably preparing a dinner to welcome the new baby, just like Mama Lolo had done for Francine three years ago.

Christelle still had a new baby's skin, so it was still too early to see if she was lighter or darker than Lucien. But she had Mama Lolo's nose and Papa Christian's mouth. Francine kept wanting to hold her but both were so small that it could not be possible. We ate dinner all together. Mama, Baba, Papa Christian and Mama Lolo were at the table with Christelle, while Lucien, Francine and I sat on the mat right next to them. Mama had made rice with pondu and sardines for us, and bugali, cikwanga, pondu and butumbutumbu for the parents. When she was cooking, Mama said butumbutumbu was good for women who had just given birth, and pondu would help her make good milk.

Christelle was a kalialia. Almost every night, we would all wake up to her crying. This happened for two months, and Baba even started to whisper about Papa Christian needing to move out. Baba was tired, yet he was not too tired to whisper it when Lucien spent the night with us. Mama, wanting her husband to get more sleep, told Mama Lolo not to go pick Christelle up when she woke up and started crying. Lucien and I did our homework by candlelight, with the smell of frying onions and Christelle crying for 20 minutes.

Before we knew it, Christelle started crawling, then sliding off the couch that Mama Lolo left her on when she was cooking. Christelle would always crawl to Lucien; even when he would stand to go to the toilet, she would follow him. We had to play a game, distracting her with toys. Lucien would place her on the table, play with her, and then throw the toy to me. Christelle would turn and crawl on the table, chasing after the toy, and Lucien would slip away. When she turned back, she would just stare quietly at the empty seat until Lucien returned.

One night, we all woke up to Christelle crying. It had been two weeks since she had last cried late at night. Mama's tactic of letting her cry had started to work. As Lucien and I sat up, unable to sleep, we heard Papa Christian shout. The books fell to the ground. Mama Lolo kept asking him to stop as it was scaring the child. More things kept falling on the ground; they sounded like heavy suitcases. Then all of it stopped, and all we heard was Mama Lolo singing Bebe Yo, Fait Dodo to Christelle. She kept pausing, but Christelle eventually stopped crying.

The next day, we did not see Mama Lolo come down in the morning to start working with Mama. Lucien did not speak the entire way to school, and though we laughed our way back, he stopped talking when we arrived at our gate. We entered the sitting room and found Christelle silent on the couch, playing with the blanket Mama Lolo had left her in. We put our bags down and greeted Mama and Mama Lolo in the back with Chikudu and Pull. Mama Lolo was wearing a long-sleeved dress and red lipstick. She quickly said she and Papa Christian had a dinner to attend when he returned. Lucien hugged her, but as he pressed on her arm, she winced. Mama explained that she had fallen on her hand from slipping on the wet floor. Her dress was not dirty.

Lucien looked at me and then at Mama, but neither of us asked any questions. Papa Christian never came home that evening and was not home by the time we slept. We didn't ask Mama Lolo about the dinner.

A week later, we woke up to Christelle crying in the middle of the night again. Papa Christian was shouting again - throwing books and suitcases on the ground. Mama Lolo was calling to him and asking him to stop. Then something started to creak, slowly at first, then faster, like a carpenter swinging a hammer to push more and more of the nail into a shelf. Like the week before, Mama Lolo was not there to wish us well at school in the morning, and Papa Christian did not play Muchuba with Baba that evening. Mama Lolo left late that evening with her red lipstick still shining and asked Lucien to help carry Christelle to their home. I did not expect Lucien to return, but I knew he did when I felt mosquitoes around my ankles.

At the end of the month, Baba came to Mama and me to tell us that Papa Christian had told him Mama Lolo was pregnant again. Christelle was only six months old. Christelle stopped crying at night. Papa Christian stopped shouting. There was no throwing of books or suitcases on the ground. Mama Lolo did not call Papa Christian or sing to Christelle. We all slept through the night. Mama did the same as when Mama Lolo was pregnant with Christelle. And every once in a while, Francine would run to sit on Mama Lolo's lap and pat her stomach. She would then pat her own stomach and ask Mama Lolo why she had a big tummy. Mama would try to chase Francine away out of embarrassment, but Mama Lolo would stop her and laugh as she tickled Francine's stomach. When she tried to explain that she had a baby in her stomach, Francine asked why Mama Lolo ate a baby when we had chickens like Chikudu. Even us, who were silently eavesdropping, broke into laughter.

Papa Christian had returned to playing Muchuba with Baba almost every evening. When Mama and Mama Lolo had finished washing the plates for the evening, Papa Christian would carry Christelle and wait for Mama Lolo by the door to their home. Mama Lolo would slowly climb the stairs until she was inside.

And almost like last time, Papa Christian came down calling for Mama. But he did so calmly with gentle knocks on our door. It was 4 a.m., but Mama was awake, completing a Novela for the day. We knocked on the door to their room, and Baba answered. He opened the door for Papa Christian, who was in a white vest with a kanga wrapped around his waist and carrying Christelle. Baba was wearing a gown given to him by an Ivorian man named Moussa Kouame. Moussa was a businessman who had come to set up his superwax shop here. Baba helped him get the papers for his business without having to pay too much money. In return, Moussa told him that men wore these gowns at home and that one could sleep easily in them even when it was really hot. Baba had hoped to get a Boubou to wear around town, but he wore the gown every night that it wasn't washed. Baba told Mama about Mama Lolo. This time, she had her slippers ready, her headscarf with holy Mary in blue, and a kikwembe wrapped at her chest above her nightgown and extending beyond her knees. Lucien and I were already in the kitchen by the time she left. Francine somehow managed to sleep through it all. She only woke up when we woke her to bathe for school an hour later.

The three of us, Lucien, Francine, and I left for school. Lucien and I wore blue navy shorts, white shirts, and blue navy ties, whilst Francine had on a white shirt, a blue navy skirt, and white socks with these things on the side that looked like the flour overflowing from the pot of bugali. We all wore black shoes. Igr. Nzabonimpa must not have eaten that day because he took out his anger on all his classes. Lucien and I had more homework to do than ever before. Lucien, being older, had more. When we got home, Lucien started walking towards the dining table, only thinking about his homework. Only when I asked if he would see Christelle and the new baby did he run out and up to Mama Lolo. Papa Christian had named him Lebon.

Lebon was not a kialalia like Christelle. He did not cry at night, but he had an appetite. Mama Lolo would feed him every two hours, and Mama had to force Mama Lolo to eat more so she would have enough milk in her breasts for Lebon. Lebon was costaud. Big cheeks with small eyes and heavy. I could not carry him for too long, even if he didn't have any problems with strangers.

For some reason, even though Christelle no longer cried at night and LeBon was true le bon in behaviour, Papa Christian started throwing books and suitcases on the floor again. It was every other week, and then every week, and then every other day, until one night, the creaking returned.

In the morning, while Lucien was bathing, I asked Mama about the creaking sound. She looked at me for a while, then came down to meet my eyes. She never explained what the creaking sound was. Instead, Mama told me how wise women are taught to use different weapons so their families can do well. Sometimes, they used prayer and song like Mama did every morning, night and when she was cleaning. Sometimes, it was through

children and what they said. It was like the way I had refused
to greet Tantine Pelou because she smelled, which embarrassed
her so much that she carried deodorant in her bag from that
day. All because of a two-year-old's honesty, yet Mama had felt
the same way even before I was born. Sometimes, a woman had
to use being a woman as a weapon. Mama explained that the
creaking we heard was just that - Mama Lolo being a woman
who brought quiet to her home. There are things parents tell us
children that we don't understand but never forget.

When Caroline was born, Lucien had just turned 12 years
old. She was born while Lucien, Francine and I were at school,
but we did not see Papa Christian until the next morning. He
had a toothpick in his mouth, a white vest and blue chequered
shorts. He had started growing a beard, and a few silver ones
would shine through. It was now different from Baba's simple
monsieur moustache and the one line below the bottom lip that
the jeune-homme of the neighbourhood were all doing. By the
time we returned from school, Papa Christian was already gone.
Mama Lolo had wrapped LeBon on her back and used another
scarf to form a pouch around her chest and stomach that Caroline would sleep in and occasionally suck on her breast when
she was hungry. Christelle sat on a brown blanket with a plastic
white-pink bowl and a pink baby spoon she used to feed herself
the Cerelac Mama Lolo had prepared. Beside her stool was a bag
filled with clothes, bottles of milk, pampers and blankets. Mama
and her would talk when one of the three children was not
interrupting them. Mama had taught Francine how to sit with
Lucien and me at a table. She also had homework to do after
school now that she was in maternelle, so she would sit through
until the candles and blue kerosene lamps were turned on. Then,
she would disappear to take care of Christelle. Lucien began to

stay at the table later and later. At times, he would finish his work around midnight, just as Mama finished washing the last pot, and Mama Lolo placed a sleeping Christelle on her right hip with LeBon still on her back and Caroline in her pouch.

Lucien packed his books into his bag, then went to carry Mama Lolo's bag. Once balanced, he peeled off Christelle, and they walked up the stairs together. Baba sat and listened to the radio. In truth, he watched them every night to make sure they entered their home safely. When I asked him why he did not help Mama Lolo and Lucien, Baba asked me how many wives he had married and left it at that. Lucien would return after a while, whisper a prayer and quietly go to sleep. We had not seen Papa Christian for weeks but heard him throwing suitcases hours after Lucien returned. Lucien seemed always to be awake before I noticed the commotion.

Mama Lolo no longer kept her hair out. She wrapped her head in silk head wraps, the way Mama did when she went to sleep or when she went to church. She no longer wore earrings. When Francine asked about her gold earrings that were round like the white balls of Mama's necklace, the ones Baba had gifted Mama on their wedding anniversary, Mama Lolo said she had given them away as Caroline and LeBon kept pulling at her ears. She wore plain coloured dresses and scarves the size of blankets around her as she carried the three children. Four months after Caroline, Mama Lolo was pregnant again. When Lucien and I were told, Lucien left quietly and returned to his homework. When school was over, I could not find Lucien the next day. When he returned, he smelt like he had bathed in a basin of butumbutumbu that Mama and Mama Lolo used to wash. He did not say anything to me but bathed and changed. He stayed at the table even past when Baba turned off his radio. When we woke up in the morning, he was gone. His bag and uniform that he had hung on the line the night before were also gone.

Francine and I met him at the gate to school. He wiped his glasses and explained that he had gone to play football with some of the class president's friends on Terrain de Deuxième Zone. After school, he bought kalanga bonbon from Mama Anna for Francine and me. We ate them quickly before we got home, wiped Francine's cheeks and promised to let her join us when Lucien and I played jeux de six. Baba had taught us Muchuba but had said that only men played this, and until then, he gave us jeux de six to play. Francine always wanted to join but would cry when she saw she was losing. We got home and went on about our homework. When it came to dinner, Mama noticed Francine did not eat as fast as she usually did. Francine ate like any other child except when it was bugali and pondu; then, she ate almost as much as me. Mama gave her the eye and called her just once. That was all it took for Francine to tell Mama of Kalanga bonbon and how Lucien and I promised to let her play Jeux de Six if she did not report us. She followed it by crying, which meant only Lucien and I would be punished. Mama brought four crates of beer next to Pululu Junior. She turned two upside down, one for each of us to kneel on and then gave the remaining two to carry above our heads until she told us to stop. She went on to finish preparing dinner for Baba. After she served him, Mama Lolo begged her on our behalf, reminding her that we still had homework to complete and we did not want Baba to hear that the children were failing in school. Mama warned us that it would be the last time we did such with her daughter. We nodded, said sorry and ran to the table before she could change her mind. Mama Lolo nodded as we ran to the table. Our punishment was not over but postponed, and she made it clear by not smiling as she watched us leave. Her red lipstick lips remained firm together.

Lucien disappeared more and more as the months went by, but always managed to be home or at school before anyone could ask him any questions. If it was not football, he was studying with Igr. Nzabonimpa in preparation for the upcoming exams. Mama Lolo was now swollen like a football and could no longer manage the three children. One day, after returning from school, we found a young woman with Mama and Mama Lolo. She was as light as Baba's brother, Ba Muloko Joseph. Mama and Mama Lolo would show her how they would cut the meat or prepare a sauce; then, they handed it over to her to try. Us children were told to call her Ya Juliette. With her in the kitchen and beside Mama Lolo, there was more time for Mama Lolo to tend to each child. Eventually, Ya Juliette began to do all the things Mama Lolo and Mama would do in the kitchen, and they would tell her what to do next from their stools. It did not take long before Ya Juliette learned all that Mama Lolo used to do and even Mama's portion. Some days after school, we would find Ya Juliette by the pots as Mama played with LeBon, Mama Lolo carried Caroline, and Christelle walked around with the doll Lucien had gotten her for her third birthday.

The year went by, except for Easter, Christmas, wedding anniversaries, and Holy Mary's Assumption day, we barely saw Papa Christian for over an hour. By now, I had learned to sleep through the nights when he threw books and suitcases. Mama Lolo did not give birth that year. Mama said it was God's will and a blessing. Mama Lolo and Mama did not speak much after that. They would sing songs together. At times, when I stood up to check on Francine and Christelle playing with Mbuwi the goat, I would see Mama Lolo closing her eyes and letting tears roll down her face as they sang songs of God. Ya Juliette would also see it but pretend to be focused on the pots. She would not sing with Mama Lolo and Mama, as they would think she was not working. Mama Lolo used to shout at Ya Juliette if she didn't work as fast as she wanted. She would remind her that she had brought her from the village, and she would send her back. When she did shout like that, Ya Juliette would also shout at Lucien, Francine, Christelle and me when the mothers were not watching.

Papa Christian's shouting at night became less clear and more muffled and slurry. Before, I could hear him clearly and understood what he was saying. But now, I only knew he was speaking before a sound like rain on a roof started, but only above our heads. It was like someone was pouring a jug of water on the floor. Caroline started crying as loud as Christelle when she was a baby. Her wails were much shorter than Christelle's, and they closely followed each other. Mama Lolo couldn't be heard, but Caroline began to calm down as the creaking sound increased. Lucien stayed sitting up even after the creaking stopped. He was gone by the time I woke up again for school. It was not that I expected him to be there, as we now only saw each other in the evening for dinner, or if he showed up early to school in the morning from football with hot bread to share with Francine and I.

Then, one evening, Ya Juliette came to sit down at the table with us. She had told the mothers she was going to the toilet. But on the way back, she sat down and asked Lucien whether he was excited about a little sibling. Lucien corrected her, reminding her of his three siblings if we were not counting Francine and I. Ya Juliette nodded but asked how Lucien would feel about having another brother. Immediately Ya Juliette asked this, and Lucien went to find Mama Lolo in the kitchen. He pulled her aside with Caroline, leaving LeBon in pampers on the mat with Christelle and Francine. Though we couldn't hear what they said, it ended with Mama Lolo slapping Lucien and pointing back to the table, where Francine and I pretended to be focused on our homework. Lucien held tears in his eyes and kept clenching his jaw, but he would let tears drop onto the tablecloth every once in a while when we were not looking. Mama Lolo was pregnant. When we went to our room that night, Lucien spoke of not wanting to be born and not wanting any other child to be born only to suffer. He kept swearing that one day, he would run away and never come back. And he did.

It was after Mama Lolo lost the pregnancy. It was after Mama Lolo had stopped wearing lipstick and started walking with a slight limp. It was after Papa Christian begged Baba to use his garden to celebrate his 15 years of marriage to Mama Lolo. Lucien only stood next to Mama Lolo at the party, even when the photographer asked him to move over to Papa Christian's side. Papa Christian and Mama Lolo danced so much at the party, only for us to wake up before the sun had risen to hear Ya Juliette carrying a woman at our door. The woman's eyes had swollen, her nose bled like a child's release of mucus, and one of her front teeth was missing. If it were not for the scarf she had used to cover her nightgown, I would not have been able to tell that it was Mama Lolo. Mama got towels, put them in warm water and washed Mama Lolo's face. She then used the same towels to press on her arms, massaging her where it hurt the most. Even though she would curl in pain, Mama Lolo did not let out any sound or scream. I knew Baba was awake because the radio that Lucien had given him was on, but he did not leave his room. These were problems for women to handle. Lucien had tried to leave after Ya Juliette explained what had happened to Mama Lolo, but Mama had held him back by asking him to hold Mama Lolo. Mama Lolo asked Ya Juliette to return and take care of the children sleeping in the house. She pulled out two mats from the corner behind the dining table and placed them on the ground by the couch. She and Mama Lolo would spend the night there using the couch pillows as sleeping pillows and the extra blankets in our cupboard.

The next afternoon, Papa Christian came to our home with many gifts for Mama Lolo, a doll and a small ball for Christelle and LeBon. He spoke for long. He told Mama Lolo that he was sorry, and he promised he would never do it again. He also apologised to Mama and Baba and then explained how ashamed he was. He swore that from that day forth, no drop of alcohol would ever touch his mouth. Baba accepted his apology, and Mama nodded to show that she stood with her husband, even though her eyes did not show the same thing. When he came to apologise, Lucien went to our room with his homework and refused to come out.

Mama Lolo returned with Papa Christian. Baba had told us that even if he was Mama Lolo's father, it was not within our tradition for one to keep a man's wife if the man himself had not thrown her suitcase out the door. Marriage was not always happy, and this was one of those times that Papa Christian and Mama Lolo had to go through together. On Sunday, we went to church together - including Lucien. Papa Christian had asked the Bishop to dedicate the mass to his marriage and family. The

Bishop and Papa Christian had known each other since primary school. Their mothers had sold vegetables next to each other in the market. When the Bishop called for Papa Christian, he came to the altar with Mama Lolo on his left side. Lucien managed to sneak away to the toilets just before the Bishop called for Papa Christian. It was almost as if he knew because he stepped away right after the gospel was finished. Ya Juliette followed Mama Lolo, carrying Caroline and walking LeBon. The six of them, Papa Christian, Mama Lolo, Ya Juliette, Christelle, LeBon, and Caroline, stood before the church as the Bishop prayed over them. When the mass ended, we found Lucien reading through his mathematics at home. Mama made Lucien sit next to her through lunch as we ate together like we had done every time a child was born. Lucien and I went to play football on Mama's orders. When we returned in the evening and prepared for bed, we heard creaking, but Papa Christian had not thrown any suitcases or shouted that night.

The next morning, Lucien, Francine, Christelle, and I woke up to Kukuruku's crowing. Mama would bathe Christelle and Francine first with the warm water from the mbabula. Then Lucien and I would follow with cold water as Mama boiled more water for Baba. When we were at the table, a loud bang happened, then another, and then fifteen more. Baba ran into the room with a wrapped towel and soap still on his chest, shouting for us to get under the table and stay quiet. Mama grabbed Francine, and Lucien grabbed Christelle, covering their mouths so they did not scream. We stayed under the table for what felt like an hour until Baba crept out from underneath the table and went to padlock the gate. He returned and closed the curtains while shouting at Francine to stop crying. He turned the radio on but put it on the lowest volume possible.

None of the channels worked for the first 45 minutes, and all we heard was the scratching sound that usually happened when Baba was changing between channels. Then, a man's voice started to speak. He addressed the people as his brothers, sisters, mothers, fathers and children. His name was General Francois Akili, and he was there to announce that Governor Kizito had been overthrown and the town was now under his leadership. Unfortunately, in the process of reclaiming the nation, the governor resisted the vision of a better country and chose to die along with his family. Baba laughed at the radio. He said that the General had killed the Governor and his family, but he could not say that on the radio because he would then have to face Bazungu and their Nations Unies.

We did not go to school the following week, and we all had to be inside the house before the sun went down. Mama and Mama Lolo used to go to the market really early and come back before 10 in the morning to avoid the many soldiers that would be on the road by lunchtime. Each time they went, they each bought food that would last us a week. By the third time they went, we had enough rice, bunga, and lenga lenga to last us at least a month. The following week, Baba heard that some soldiers had tortured, killed and left the Bishop's body in the centre of town for a full day. Papa Christian came down that night to play Muchuba and talk about how the soldiers had disgraced his friend. It was seminarians who later collected his body from the streets. Every day, we would see families walking towards the border. Mothers carrying all they could on their heads in a big ball of several kikwembe tied together, and a child on their back. Baba said things would go back to normal. Two weeks passed, then three, and then four. Almost nothing changed, except for

General Akili announcing that schools would reopen and be free for all children, including girls. Baba said the General was trying to make sure that the Bazungu didn't kill him like they had helped him kill Governor Kizito. We were not allowed to go to school - Baba refused.

Because Papa Christian could not go far and many jobs had now closed, he would spend every other evening that he was not playing with Baba at the bar Chez Sami on our street. One night, when Papa Christian was drinking with other men at Chez Sami, Lucien gave me a bracelet. It was made of copper with a flat part for the back of the wrist and two small round balls, one on each end, that rested on either side of the nerves that led to my palm. My name was written on the flat part. He showed me his. It was exactly the same with his name on it.

In the morning, Papa Christian passed by to ask Baba to escort him to the Bishop's funeral. General Akili had finally allowed for him to be buried. It would not cause any protests or draw any attention from the Bazungu. Baba wore his Black suit and carried an envelope he would give to the Bishop's sister. A few hours after they left, Mama Lolo sent Ya Juliette to town to buy some meat for the fathers to eat in the evening. Once Ya Juliette left, she asked Lucien to pack some clothes and shoes for him and Christelle. When Mama asked her what the children were packing for, Mama Lolo said they were headed to Papa Christian's village, where they would be safer. She said that she could not risk losing another pregnancy, and with soldiers in the town, she did not want to risk it. Mama nodded, hugged her, reached inside her chest next to her breast and gave her some money to buy LeBon water on the way to the village. Mama called Francine and me to say our farewell. I hugged Mama Lolo

and the younger ones, but Lucien and I shook hands like we had
seen Baba and Papa Christian do - like men. It was then that
Lucien left.

When Papa Christian came back, Ya Juliette served him as
Mama served Baba. It was only after he had finished eating that
he asked where Caroline and Mama Lolo were. Before Mama
responded, Francine shouted that Mama Lolo had gone to the
village because she was pregnant. Papa Christian asked Mama if
this was true, and Mama had said that Mama Lolo had told her it
was Papa Christian's idea. He got up and started running but did
not get very far when he remembered the soldiers outside and
came back to sit down with Baba. Baba did not move or speak,
and his eyes remained fixed on Mama.

Francine and I returned to school in the fifth week of General
Akili's regime. Mama told me to avoid the roads by Palais du
Gouverneur; instead, we walked by the lake to avoid soldiers.
I was never to let go of Francine's hand and she was never to
leave my side except when we were in class. Lucien never came
back. None of them did. Baba had tried to help Papa Christian
by asking soldiers to look for his children, but after a week, they
told him the children could not be found. They never returned,
even when Papa Christian started having other children, even
when Ya Juliette became Mama Dada. Even when Baba's first
daughter came to live with us after her mother passed in a market stampede, I thought Lucien would come back after General
Akili died. He did not.

Even now, as I left Terrain du Deuxième Zone, I kept my
ears open in case Lucien managed to return and decided he was
going to play football. Mama Dada had once said that Mama Lolo

had lied about being pregnant so we would not suspect her plan to leave Papa Christian. It was also possible that the pregnancy she had claimed to lose may have also been a lie. If this plastic stick had been there with us back then, maybe Lucien would still be here today. Maybe we could have been playing Muchuba like Baba and Papa Christian, but he would not chew leaves like Papa Christian chewed.

Someone somewhere was having a child soon. Do they want it? Did they want it in the first place? What was the price for it? What was Mama Lolo's?

~ Three ~

CROSSROADS

"See. Hear. Touch. Taste.
Smell. The dark shall be here
for you soon. Tell me, child,
what do you see?"

When the darkness came, we kept the sun. Hid it among and between us and made love—the kind of love of an old grandfather dancing merengue without breaking a sweat. The type of love made only on the dance floor when the five-drum beat in Magic System's Premier Gaou drops, and strangers tighten their belts, take off their heels, hang up their call, and forget their smoke. The love in the exhale of nostalgia as it's followed by the voices of Brick & Lace's Love is Wicked. And in the heat in the faceoff to Crime Mob's Knuck If You Buck. Knees twisting, waist whining, elbow popping - not the worm. We did not know each other. At least not in this life. And yet, love was made when the tall man in red with blue locs hit the same beats, the same move and the same energy as the short woman in the green skirt, long nails, dull gold ring and the Maasai Kenyan flag bracelet. We hid the sun in between the jumping, the screams of disbelief, the laughter and the two running away with tears of joy. They would be back the same way they left, as a Bald man in white shoes stepped forward to Krump. As he stumped it out, a purple lace-topped, knee-high boot-wearing, nose-pierced being duck-walked through the chants flew into the air that the tall man had to look up and landed effortlessly into a dip. We were living.

"And what of you, elder? What do you hear?"

A six shakes differently from a five, as does it from a three and from a one. The man who does not know this will sit on the edge of his seat, and his bum bum will press into the plastic so it creaks. And every time he is past the cup, the hand will first wish-wash-fish-fash on the trouser, trying to wipe the previous misfortune or calm the leg, pressing the ground every ten seconds. At this time, there are no whispers, so the emptiness is filled from the corner by a man with an accent telling the day's news. He is interrupted ever so often by the exhalation of the wind that shakes the wooden legs holding the voice. When his voice is lost completely, someone will bang the back of the black plastic until the click of a battery falling in place is heard. The dented silver rod on the side will be twisted and pulled, releasing a squeak ever so often like a man does when he is told to stand on feet that have walked too many days.

Beside the fisha-fasha trouser man is a father chewing what he calls bitter leaf, but his gums collide like an axe on firewood. Bitter leaf today, groundnut yesterday, before that maize—even the goat was resting. His chewing stopped only when he was swallowing, and that one, too, was like the engine that broke down after two days of carrying men, women, a newborn child, a mattress and chickens. That was back when the General shot the Commander. Since then, he has been chewing and swallowing. Chewing and swallowing everything. His was that one of rain hitting tin roof but never landing on the soil. Wiping the side of his mouth like a fork whisking eggs for children's omelette, he turns to the fisha-fasha trouser man as he shakes a four—two short of being safe. The fisha-fasha trouser man exhales like a taxi man stuck in ten-minute traffic and trying to think of a shortcut. He does not hear the swallowing or the clearing of the throat, but he inhales in time to hear a question. Before he answers, he laughs, and that is already a response. The fisha-fasha trouser man is hearing what is being said, but his youthfulness does not allow him to listen. His hums, yes and ok, are rushed and out of place, quickly leaving his tongue, and yet through all the chewing and swallowing, a father continues to insist. Their conversation is the sound of tyres swallowed by mud and forced to continue accelerating. A father tries to warn a man, but the man sees himself as better and does not listen. The fisha-fasha trouser man does not know that the man he pities in between his laughter and politeness used to be him. The fisha-fasha trouser man is not chewing or swallowing today, but there is much time left for him and none for me to waste on it. One groundnut, one bitter leaf, one maize at a time. The past can choke a man into silence.

"Can you smell that?"

Taxis are different from buses. It still holds the sweat of the hustle and grind of everyday people trying to make their way from one destination to another. In a bus, all sweat comes to you at once, mixed like a stew made from leftover beans, goat meat, cabbage, and carrots. You can tell they are all present, but they have become inseparable. In a taxi, the sweat is from the driver and their toil. Sweat that had seeped into the chairs from hours where he parked his car under a tree left a slit-like opening at the top of the window on his side and laid back his chair. He would take this chance to rest as he waited for the next wave of customers, but the heat would still reach him, even with his blue short-sleeved shirt open and his white vest untucked. When his phone would ring, he would wake up with a back wet and a chair moist with his imprint. As he hung up, he would put his shoes back onto his swollen feet and let these new socks cook themselves into the sweat.

Others sometimes left a scent to linger—perhaps a kindness to keep company with the taxi man until the next customer. Another woman was here before me. She had sat on the left side, and now she had trickled to the right. Her lotion was stronger than her perfume. It was the kind of lotion not bought by scanning a barcode and paid for with cash. She probably wore a ring or two that was made out of bronze or copper and then painted Gold. She may have flaunted it off to others, and some would marvel at her collections whilst others would see the dullness of the gold but not stop her. On a hot day like today, the mind had to travel to forget the fresh dust the air conditioner coughed in. Cold dust tickles the hairs of the nostrils differently. It sits comfortably, locking one arm to the hair and using the other to taunt a request for freedom. Escaping the air conditioning meant opening the windows and being filled with the thick fumes from the exhaust pipes of water tanks and the farmer bringing his over-packed Toyota truck of cassava to town.

The taxi driver knew best to park the car 15 houses away from mine, and even if we both knew where I lived, he let me play this game of protecting myself from possible danger. A paper that had passed from hand to hand to purse to wallet to bra and then to hand was now passed over his shoulder. I stepped out right by where a black nylon had been thrown four days ago and now clogged the drainage system. The grey-greenish brown water was rising, and from it stepped out Omo from the uniforms a mother washed, faeces from a woman who had been sent diarrhoea by a jealous relative and could not contain it, and urine from a man that had only eaten bread and drowned it with anything that had a percentage on the bottom of the bottle. It danced on top of the cow dung and goat droplets that littered the dry grass of the children's football field. Only the rains could quiet them. When each drop kissed the earth, the richness that came would soothe, bring peace and a lot of snores. For now, I followed the trace of onions—placed over a fire with oil. It was a guide home and a key to the engine of my stomach. When last did I eat? At the gate, I quietly opened the door, trying to hide in the shadows of the kerosene. Someone had left a cooling pot ajar, and freshly boiled maize trickled out. Had Baba offered the man wearing Adidas sport deodorant as cologne our maize?

"How about you? Do you feel anything?"

Batista reverses Undertaker's Tombstone piledriver with a spinebuster. Jaws are clenched, and someone is gripping someone's wrist tight. They were both out for blood! Batista goes in for the count, but Stone Cold Steve Austin only gets two. Batista rolls to one knee, trying to think of how to keep the Dead Man down, only for Undertaker to wake up from the dead and stare at him. Batista is in shock! And right before they get up, another power cut. All of us children burst into anger at the mystery power company that decided to cut power right on the cusp of this match. Someone continues the story of the fight, saying that Undertaker finished Batista with the Last Ride and won the title from Batista. Another cousin refuses and says Undertaker got tired, and Dave "The Animal" Batista delivered a Batista Bomb to hell. One, two, three, ding ding ding, and the winner is your World Heavyweight Champion, Batista. As they go back and forth, the aunt in the corner holds perfectly still, her mouth parting ever so gently in time to the fierce holding of the Rosary. Her spirit is unmoved by the commotion, but she confides in prayer in the hope that the power would return so she could see whether Don Pedro Jose Donoso will reveal the truth to Isabel. In truth, with all the prayer she did, she could not resist the man that was Salvador Cerinza.

When the power did not return, disappointment hung as the older sisters followed their hands down the hallway to a light brown wooden shelf where the matchsticks rested on the top shelf, along with the blue metal kerosene lamps. Mama had put it there after one of the brothers had tried to light the lamps as a child. The sisters also brought the candles. Reluctantly, the children lined up to take the different lamps—one behind the house to the kitchen where the Mamas sat on their stools with babies sleeping on their backs; one for the babas who were mumbling about the new president's speech that the radio just played; and one on the table by the aunt who was praying. The candles would go on the dining table, and two would be placed in a metal bowl by the shower door and the toilet door. The children would rush back with excitement because Kaka would be shuffling the cards, and if you were not at the table once he was done, even Dada would not be able to speak for you. The rules were simple: you either won or made sure you had the lowest cards.

King, Queen and Jack were ten, the command card was 25, and Joker - the revenge card - was 50. If you lost, everyone else had to slap your hands until you gave up or dodged their slap. So when the cry babies wanted to join, Kaka stared at Dada in nervousness whilst the rest of us tried to force them to go into a corner and play with dolls. Dada just nodded and let them play. One of them lost, we all laughed, and the slaps began—until one brother got excited and delivered a hot one that sent the poor baby crying to his mother. After getting our ears pulled and kneeling, we went back to the cards, but this time, we brought a tall glass and a jug of water. In their anger, the older sisters and brothers made each of us younger siblings lose at least twice. Every time a child moved, they felt the water jiggle in their stomach. They tried to think about anything but water, peeing and the bathroom. Until the game was finally over, they could not ease themselves. One of the brothers had taught some of us the trick of not squeezing our legs too tight and slowing down our movement and breathing.

The game started to slow down, and we eventually lost interest or wanted the game to end so we could rush to the toilet or outside at the far corner of the house to release ourselves. When we would come back, Dada and the sisters would be gone to help in the kitchen. A young uncle, working but yet to marry, came and sat with us. He would tell us stories. Stories of places where stairs moved on their own and you could enter a box and it would take you to the sky. We would ask questions. Has he been in one of them before? How did he get there? Could he take us with him next time? He said he would take us if we behaved. Otherwise, Karashika would come and take the bad children away. One child, who had only started leaving his mother's side to play with other children, would ask what a Karashika was. The rest of us would whisper to each other, knowing Uncle was about to tell us the story of his neighbour that Karashika took. The neighbour was a bad child. They fought with others, did not greet their elders and didn't help in the house. They did not study and would break things. So one day, Karashika came from the river beside Uncle's neighbour's house. She used her power to walk through the wall into the neighbour's bedroom whilst they were sleeping. She used her powers and began to suck the spirit out of the child, but it so happens that night, the neighbour's mother went to check on her child. When she entered the room, Karashika ran away, scared off by the bible in the mother's hand and left the child with only half their spirit. The neighbour was never the same again. As the uncle finished the story, the younger children's eyes were wide with fear. Some children will have nightmares tonight. Before Uncle could continue, Baba's first daughter walked into the house with her bag, and Uncle got up to say hello. Baba's first daughter had told Mama she did not like Uncle because he wore bad perfume, so we always pinched our noses behind Uncle's back whenever they met.

The other sisters came to the dining table with three big trays of Ugali, three sauces with small pieces of goat meat and a lot of spinach, and six smaller plates with Ugali, big pieces of goat meat and some spinach for Baba, Baba's two friends, Uncle, Aunty who was praying, and Baba's first daughter. The mamas would eat their own from the pot as they started preparing what they would cook for tomorrow. Three children would run to give Baba and his two friends their food. Aunty would stand up and wait till they came back, and then she would pray. She would pray for the food, pray for Baba's first daughter's work, pray for one of the mamas who was pregnant, pray for all the children in school, pray for Uncle to get married, pray for the peace of the world, pray for the poor, pray for our families in the village, across the world—she would then pray for those who were less fortunate. When she first started praying for the food, we all used to close our eyes, but then we would finish the prayer and find meat missing from the trays. Now, most of us keep our eyes open and say Amen and dig in before we even sit down. As siblings, we were divided into older teenagers, younger teenagers, and kids. Sometimes, the older teenagers took the slow-eating young children with them so that they would make sure they were eating. You had to eat fast; you put something in your mouth before you swallowed the last thing; the taste wasn't important. And you never turned your head when Kaka told you there was a rat behind you because your piece of goat meat would disappear when you looked.

Some sisters took the trays to the kitchen, whilst some went with the other children to say goodnight to the Babas before going to the shower and bathing the youngest children. In an hour, all the children except Kaka and Dada would have showered, prayed and slept. Kaka would then walk around the compound making sure the goats were correctly tied and the gate was locked well. Dada and Baba's first daughter would help the mamas wash the pots, pans and plates. Aunty would be praying, and the babas would still listen to the radio, talking and playing. It would be at least another two hours before anyone checked on the children sleeping to see if any had urinated on the bed or if there was time to save the bed sheet from being soaked from the waters that had been drunk. For those two hours, no one would feel the absence of a restless child who snuck through the window onto the avocado tree and climbed over the fence behind the house.

"Do you hold your tongue? Or does it carry something else?"

When the children got tired of playing football or "Mummy and Daddy", one of them would climb the tree. It had to be the lightest so the branch would not break. The rest would wait at the bottom with their shirts or skirts held out to catch the avocado that would shake off. When they got enough, they ran to eat them behind the goats so that we, the mamas, would not see them, and the skin would be eaten or trampled on before we could realise. Or so they thought. They spat on the avocado and then wiped it to clean it. With no knives, they had to peel the sandpaper-like skin aside before biting into the soft green-yellow. By the end, all that was left was the seed and skin. As children do when they think they are smarter than those who brought them into the world. They thought they would hide the seeds by digging shallow holes and placing them there. Then, all of a sudden, all our children would have uncontrollable thirst. Drinking water would wash their mouths to hide the green and cleanse the tongues for the plantain with chicken and mayonnaise.

When it was plantain and chicken day, some of the children tried to pretend to be sick. They would eat soil to create a bland taste in their mouth when their tongue touched the gums. They would take less water across the day to make their spit think their tongue tasted clammy, like a child with a fever. When the mamas made them drink tea with ginger, lemon, and garlic, they would gulp it down without flinching. Because if they did, then they were not sick. Only a few ever made it past Mama to get their full plate of plantain and chicken - to heal them back to good health. Ere sick, you couldn't laugh, so when something was funny, you coughed, making sure enough mucus was pulled from the nose into the throat and mouth.

If a child continued to be sick, we would take aloe vera from the field and break it. They would put its juice into hot water and make the child drink it. Children have their games, and so do we. Mama Dada and I would look at each other and smile with our eyes. We would give them aloe vera tea, then onion juice, and watch the child try to keep their body from shivering. By the evening, the child would have healed, whether they were sick in the first place or not. The children would run around until I told Kaka to turn on the TV to make them sit in one place. Mama Dada and I didn't care what was on TV so long as no child was crying. But then the power was cut, and almost within thirty minutes, a child came crying that they had been slapped. Mama Dada was cutting onions for the stew with goat meat because I could no longer bend forward. She would tease me with charcoal she was about to add to the fire, and I would laugh but take one and chew. I had learned to find the soft crack with my teeth that would break its hardness into soft crumbs like cassava flour. We cut the meat pieces tiny as the drought was coming, and this goat was not giving any newborns any soon. The children were getting restless, but I taught Kaka how to manage them. The sisters would come soon to get the food—at least, what we had not eaten to see if the food was ready. A way to defeat children who do not want to sleep is to let Ugali sit in their stomachs. The weight will send their bodies naturally to a pillow.

We would wipe the pots with the remaining Ugali and swallow. Mama Dada would find a toothpick to dig out the meat between her teeth. We would pass the pots between us; she would wash them, I would dry them, and when Dada and Baba's first daughter would come, they would put them away. Mama Dada would have chewed the toothpick like it was sugarcane. When Mama Dada and I made it to bed, everyone else would be asleep. But we would not change it; the time between us allowed us women to be, even if it meant we ate the cold watered Nido with cereal or the half-eaten buttered bread. We would not want to sit with the men who would talk about what they would have become if the General had not done what he did. Every day and the same. When they first started, I would swallow the salt in my tears every night, but now I just laughed at what we had become and then lay down next to the man snoring beside me.

Smoke from charcoal travels to your throat through your eyes. As they water, the smoke builds up in your throat and lands on your tongue through coughs. Smoke from kerosene does not do the same as charcoal. It will reach through your nose, drown your tongue and through to your stomach.

"Come—step forward—one behind the other. When the darkness comes, do not run. If you feel you cannot tell it what you have just told me. Certainly, it is here for you."

~ Four ~

PENANCE

This is all I will ever have to
say to you.

Doudou,

I wonder if someone still calls you that now, or if you let that one remain ours, Christian. This letter is not an apology. Many times in the years after that, I thought of you and thought I could have written a letter. This is not that letter, and I doubt that letter will ever come.

This letter is an introduction. It serves to introduce you to my grand-daughter, Louise. A stubborn, headstrong, and loving young girl. She has been working on a project about family and family history that started as a small school project. She has chosen to come find you against her father's will and my initial refusal. In her mind, you are an important part of her family history; otherwise, she would never have existed. She is right. Without you, Louise would have never existed. But she is also wrong. If I had remained your wife, Louise might still have been born, but she may not have had a grandmother to tell her all about her father. The man you were when I left my father's house could have been her Tate. Still, the man you became by the time Akili killed Kizito and your friend Benjamin Mugabo can never be her Tate.

She will ask you many questions until you are tired. Do not hide any-thing from her. Her father has not hidden anything about you, and neither have I. If you hide something or try to lie, she will know. She has my mother's sense, the same sense that warned me about marrying a man from Nyansima, and I did not listen. Do you remember that?

How you used to take a different road to work at the butchery just so you and I could talk as I rushed to school. You would let me go to enter school just before Prefet Tembo would have made me mop. We would stop at the corner so no one would see us, especially Sœur Chantal. You would hold my hand and swear we would change the country together. We would start in Beke. You would get a job in the government, and when I finished my degree, you promised to help me find a job. Our money would build houses, schools, and other businesses. The people would love us so much that they would vote for you as governor. Then you would be President, and I, your Première Dame. Our sons would be named after me, and our daughters after you.

Florence and I used to giggle and sango whenever I told her what you said. There were times when she would forget to hide her jealousy and would tell me she wished she had a man who loved her like my Christian. We didn't know then you were an ékonda of a man - so beautiful to look at but terrible for the body.

When Baba refused you, I listened to you. I believed you when you said that Baba was worried that you would die like many of his friends did when they fought for a revolution. He was no longer a young man and only wanted the best for his daughter, but his fear, you said, blinded him from seeing our destiny. A child learns to walk and forgets the father used to run.

I cried for weeks to Mama, and she would sit in silence until I finished, then she would remind me that Baba was a man, and he would show me a real man for me. I would soon forget about the rubbish boy who wore nice trousers and put on perfume like the Beke women who came for funerals. Mama warned that you were a man who loved himself too much and would not know how to take care of a woman. I would tell her you know how to take care of me like Baba took care of her. Mama whispered how you would leave me naked for the whole village to see so long as you shined.

When I came to you, you would tell me stories of friends you knew who had left our village and were now rich in Beke and Kinshasa. You were just waiting for me to finish school, then we would go to Beke to start our life together and make our dreams for our country come true. And you waited. Florence and I would go study, and you would join us as we

talked about the history for hours, then answered Prof. Lubenja's soci-
ology questions. Mama and Baba thought I forgot about you through it
all. Mama would ask Mama Nyabadeux's eldest to help her carry her
bison to our house, Baba would invite Papa Jean-Jean to dinner with his
sons, and at night, after prayer, they would mention the good families
that were well respected with good children in the village. When Baba
saw that no other man had caught my eye, he gave me one month, or
he would marry me off.

I begged you to come back and try again. I went on my knees for you
to speak to my father, and Florence joined me just to get you to agree.
When Baba chased you out, and Mama did not fight for me, we ran
away. I packed the rosary Tate gave me and all the clothes I could carry
to Florence to give to you. Mama had stood by her husband, and I stood
by mine. We arrived in Beke, but not the city you promised we would
live in. You took us to squeeze into Mohamed's house with his four
children. Be patient, I told myself, even after I got pregnant. I still believed you would stop working at the butchery, and your friends would
get you a job in the government. When I was about to give birth, you
finally listened to me begging you again for a place of our own. Even
then, it was one month before we moved into our small home in Zone
Industrielle. Mohamed would call you to join him in working different
jobs for two weeks, four months and sometimes six months. Somehow,
those jobs managed to pay the rent and provide enough food for you to
eat. For your son, I had to use some of the money you gave me to buy
small things I could sell. I would laugh when you would beat your chest
in front of other men because of how big your son was becoming. I never
spoke about the watch you bought. We stayed in Zone Industrielle for
seven years, and I prayed because God would not shame me.

One Sunday morning, I woke you up to go to church so we could pray
for doors to open. You rose, slapped me, and returned to sleep. I took

our son and walked to Cathédrale with all the other women. I stayed in Cathédrale even after the mass and prayed the rosary from start to finish. I left it to God and came home to cook for you. I met you by the door wearing a grey suit with all our things by your feet. Before I could start to ask what was happening, whether Papa Cyprien had forced us out even after I had paid him the rent balance or if you were chasing me away, you turned me around. You placed a gold necklace on my chest. Then, in my palm, you put the matching earrings. You had found a place for us to live. It was not on La Belle Ave, but it was close enough to be able to see it.

As men, you think you are the smartest and that only your way is right. And because of fear, we women would sit and agree for peace of mind, but the day we didn't, men like you did not even know. When I decided to leave, it was Da Sarah who helped me without asking. She is the one who sold my earrings and necklace. Yes, the woman who sat and laughed with you as you bought her beers is the same woman who helped me escape. She sold them to Igr. Nzolantima. Remember, at the time, he had been trying to find ways to keep his marriage alive. I still pray that those earrings brought blessings for him and Emmanuella.

Parting from those earrings was a blessing, not immediately, but where I stand today, I could have never done so without selling those earrings. It was not an easy blessing like the way you and I met at Da Solange's wedding. There was no one to turn to when I walked my children to the border. Yes, my son was becoming a man and very much had been the father to his brother and sisters, but even then, he still looked to me. It was not the same as running away to Beke with you for our dreams and love, knowing we would have each other to lean on. There were no dreams to be chased.

A shegue's life can sometimes be better than the life the children and I had to live. Shegues are in their own country and know the language of the land. And yet, the Lord works in mysterious ways. As we entered Rwanda after three hours of standing in line, a woman and her family approached me and stayed with me the entire way so that all I carried were my children front and back.

We all learned to carry bags of cement and stones, pick up rubbish on the road, and share mikate between us for lunch and dinner. We each did our part to bring food, especially for Celine. Her brothers would find avocado trees and steal enough for Celine to have milk. At night, we would take turns going into some farms to pluck some sombe. We couldn't take much, and I taught the children how to cut it so it would look like insects and animals had eaten the leaves.

When a man's voice passed our door, I used to reach for my waist. A man would lift his arm faster than I could see; I would hold my waist. In their voices, all I heard was volume. It did not matter if they laughed or shouted; I held my waist. I would feel their voices vibrate through me, and I would hold tight just below where five children had been carried. The stomach you had said was too big for a woman who respects herself was the same stomach I used to hold the knife Da Sarah gave me when I gave her your ring. She had used it to save her Sami. It was the last thing her husband had given her before he was killed. A French man he had met in Abidjan had given it to him as a gift for managing to close a deal that would see many African countries grow. Bazungu had funny gifts. Da Sarah warned that a woman must be wise because men were stupid. She looked at me like an older sister, a friend like my Florence used to look at me. The knife she gave me was to make sure that I did not leave a demon for the devil. And every time a man approached, my hand held that knife.

I have come close to killing two men before. One was a complete stranger, and the other was the brother-in-law to the woman I met at the border.

Twenty-two years ago, you left for a funeral, and I left for my life. At the time, it was the hardest thing to do. You, Doudou, were all I had, and I put all of myself into you. Where else could I go? My parents would never accept me after choosing a man over them. And no one in the BaNidunga would have helped me in fear of my parents. Before leaving you, leaving them was the hardest thing I ever did, and I thought that once I left, I would never have to leave again. And yet, I did leave once again because of you.

What I did was love, and I put love into making our home. I cannot speak for you, and if you could explain it as love, then I fear for the person you hate just as much as you loved me. Between you and I, we made five children; you only saw four of them and did not know any of them. As you bought suits and watches and spent more time in bars, you knew that the children you had given life to were now working to pay for the food you ate when you were not chewing bitter leaf. We made children together. We wore our rings to show our promise to each other, for better or for worse. You were never a husband. You were never a father.

If you were a father but a poor husband, my children would not have changed the names they inherited from you. If you still believe that your children will carry your legacy through having your name, that hope, that dream, much like ours, will forever be just a dream.

Lucien was the first to change his name to his father's name - Muder-hwa. It is he who made me a Tate when he married a Ugandan girl with a mwanya - Eva Nansubuga. Lucien and Eva's marriage has blessed me with a sister and another mother to spend days raising children like I used to do with Da Marie and Mama Kaka before her. Louise is their first child and is as hardworking and determined as her father. He wakes up and goes to work before sunrise but makes sure to return before sunset to sit with his children until they fall asleep. How many times did you sit with Lucien?

Christelle now works as a lawyer with organisations that protect women from violence. She has devoted her life to protecting other women from men like you, and she works with other powerful women like Mama Phina, Winnie Byanyima, Pheona Nabasa, and Shamim Malende.

With the help of their father, LeBon completed his Bachelors at Makerere University in some technology thing that me I never understood. He worked for MTN for two years and then got a scholarship to do his masters in the USA. He then managed to find a scholarship for his girlfriend, Bénédicte, to complete her degree. They are both in Michigan, and they sent us many pictures of them in the snow on WhatsApp and Facebook. Bénédicte, or Da Bebe as we call her, is a good young woman who I got to see grow from a young girl with so much pain. We had our pain and being filles Beke in common. She was already a daughter to me, but when she finishes her degree, LeBon and his father agreed he will marry her.

Caroline is really Louise's mentor. She is the artist of the family. She used to draw and write beautiful stories in Beke as a child. She was a very quiet child, but she was the one who used to sow her sisters and brothers' clothes. She studied journalism, then worked for one of the church radios and wrote for New Vision Newspaper at the same time. She left those jobs to work for NTV, turning research into interesting news for their Uganda channels. Her work is her focus, and many men do not know how to talk to a smart woman. I see her sometimes forget she does not need a man to feel complete in what she is doing, and I remind her that waiting can be a blessing. She does not want to live the life I lived.

Celine is a sharp child. She learned from her brothers and sisters, and they were strict with her. She didn't live under you, so she had no memories of fear, and her older brothers and sister would see her relax too much. I gave birth to her, but it is them who raised her, and now she travels all over the world receiving awards and meeting other young Africans eager to change their communities. She is now a Mandela Washington Fellow as she designs school curricula to help schools in poor and refugee communities perform better. She might meet the President of the African Development Bank this year, Akinwumi Adesina and his wife Grace Adesina.

The Adesina, I look at them and their story and sometimes think of us. We used to talk about the roads we would fix, the schools we would improve, and the pride we would bring to our people. And that we would do all of it together, side by side. We could have done so many things if we followed those dreams together. Christian and Louise Lugogo - The Lugogo. Mama Kaka used to say we were a beautiful couple when we first moved into her apartment and that we would go far. I just needed to keep praying. She stopped saying it the third time she heard you screaming my name and throwing my body onto the ground.

When you were fast asleep, Mama Kaka would come to our door with a towel and hot water mixed with vixie. She would not say anything as she pressed my wrists, shoulder, neck, face, and eyes. When I would scream, she would cover my mouth and wait to see if you would come. When you did not, she would whisper that screaming would encourage a husband to beat a wife even more. I needed to learn to stay quiet so as not to make you angry.

I used to see your sweetness and softness because carrying, beating, and cutting meat at the butchery made you too tired.

As a mother, I know enough to know that even with all the love I could give my children, my sons, Lucien and LeBon, would need their father. If they lived day by day, seeing what you did to me, they would grow into men who did the same because they would have learned that it was the normal and expected thing to do as a man. To be absent; to eat, drive, and bathe in alcohol; to beat their wives like they were pounding sombe; and once beaten, their wives' clothes would be torn and their insides beaten as well. After finishing their exercise, they would leave their wives on the floor and collapse into bed, sleeping like a well-breastfed baby. The following day, they would wake up singing Franco, N'Yoka Longo, or Koffi as they sat for breakfast their bruised wives had prepared with tears and prayer pleas. The number of times I have said "Mungu Baba nipe nguvu." Their wives would also lose count of suffering at the hands of their husbands. Husbands who had learned that this was love from their father. Living in our house, Lucien and LeBon would have done one of two things - kill their wives or kill you.

The next day, when you came back home, I stopped speaking. You did not realise the difference. You did not realise that Lucien's clothes were no longer in the house, nor was he.

When he was younger, Lucien thought that his staying and living with Kaka was because there were no other children between Mama Kaka and me. When Mama Kaka and I both gave birth, he believed it was because Kaka needed an older brother to be an example. And because he believed it, Lucien never let himself drop from being among the top two in all his classes. He would check Kaka's homework to make sure that he was also doing the right thing. An omission of the truth made

Lucien a big brother to all the other children who came after him. But what is done in the dark shall come to light.

One night, you nearly ended my life. When you had finished and I was sure you were sleeping, I went to Mama Kaka for help. Lucien managed to find us in Mama Kaka's sitting room before she could finish helping me reduce the swelling. Children are very smart and will pretend to not know something for the sake of the adults around them. He never spoke about it.

A man's success depends on the public silence of the woman or women around him. Each time my body would swell, Mama Kaka would remind me that talking to people would do me no good. It would bring shame to you as a man, and that shame would be transferred to my children. What kind of mother willingly brought shame onto their children? Instead, I was to be more of a woman. Be more beautiful to remind you of why you married me. And appease you by using my womanhood. Mama Kaka explained that is how she got Francine. But even a woman's magic can fail. There was not enough red lipstick to hide the blood in my eyes. And even carrying your child was no longer enough to bring peace and protect me. If one day I slept peacefully, the next I would taste blood. Even when you knelt before God and the Bishop, you ignored the vows for better and increased for worse. Was that night after we celebrated our marriage in front of the Bishop the first night you found happiness in between Juliette's legs?

You are, after all, a stupid man who only knew how to dress well, and I was a silly girl who did not see that. You have lied. You have broken me. You have scarred me. You have scarred my children. You nearly killed me, and even then, I would not have left you. But to suffer all of that and then learn I was to become a first wife raising another woman's child you made in my home. *Mama Kaka agreed that staying would have killed us all.*

Children give parents joy and strength. Lucien knew of all the things you did to me, but his plan was to step into your roles and be the man you never managed to become. It was Christelle who made me leave. She asked if she was to get married, would she also have to be beaten by her husband. We were washing plates with Mama Kaka, and as women with the wisdom of what life has taught us, we did not respond to her but said she would find a good man. And she has because she has had a father who has shown her what a good man is. I cannot hate you, even with all you did, because it brought me to where I am today. To a husband—with him, we have built enough for us, our children, and their children. A man whom I have dreamt with, and who wakes up every day to fulfil his promise as a whole. With him, our dreams are no longer just dreams. Mama Kaka spoke of a woman's silence as a protector of a man's reputation, but my husband has shown me that a wife's voice has the power to give a man more strength. I don't think you will ever know this. I just pray you were kinder with Juliette.

I wish you no ill will. I hope you have learned or are learning to be a better man, but I doubt you have changed much. I want you to know that I forgive you, not for your sake, but for mine. I forgive you for all the things that you did. I can never forget it, and still, I forgive you. But do not be mistaken; your claim to me, my children, and their children ended the day I left you. Do not think that by talking to Louise, you will find a way to be a part of us again. Tell the child your truth and everything you want her to believe, then let her return to her Shangazi, and you return to chewing your bitter leaf. Anything more than that will only be possible in your dreams—and we both know how many of those come true. Louise knows this, and now you do, too.

This is all I will ever have to say to you.

Louise Muhigirwa

~ Five ~

LEGITIMATE

Do you have any last
requests?

Because we share the same blood, it does not make us brothers and never will. You were born and lived without anything to worry about. Every night, you slept with a full stomach, and when you did fall hungry, it was never for too long. Do you even know the cost of flour? Do you know the price of salt? You just eat what you are served with no questions of how it arrived on your table and who suffered so you could eat goat meat. Can you even kill a goat? I will show you how you kill one.

I will put a hole in you. We will place hooks into your feet and pull on the ropes so your feet face the sky and your head faces the ground. Through the hole, we shall drain you of every drop of blood. When the blood has filled the pot, we will pour salt into it and place it aside. On your chest, at the centre, I will open your skin with the mark of your cross. I will put my hands inside and feel between the meat that holds your ribs and the skin that covers them. Then I will cut. Cut away the skin from your ribs, your arms, and your back. I will leave the skin on your ankles and your wrists. These we will cut off from the rest of you and roast with your head. We will pull the skin away, and fat will fall along with the shit you are holding right now trying to be a man. See, there is no way that both of us can live by the end of today. It is either you or me. And you have had your time. Something that was given to you. As for me, all you see around you now - I built, worked for, and sacrificed. You know nothing of this.

Your father dressed you in the best clothes and fed you well until your cheeks were swollen. He sat with you and his wife at the front of the church. My father would only see me early in the morning when the grasshoppers and crickets could be heard or late at night in some corner where men like you would go to find women who were not their wives. They fed you before school. My father paid just enough for me to sit on a bench with ten other children and watch them eat porridge. And then you went to university with a suitcase full of food and the best shoes bought by your father. My father did not have the money to send me to the university in the unfinished building in Zone Industrielle. Instead, he sent me to join the army. To make my country proud and protect its people. And I fought because my father had told me it was the biggest honour to fight and defend one's country. Because that is what a man is supposed to do. When I returned, my mother was gone. Buried with nothing to show for a name. Where was I? Protecting her from enemies she never knew of or cared for because of my father. All that protecting, for her to die on the streets in an accident with a moto.

We have met before. You sat eating biscuits and reading as I was told to return to fight and honour my mother. Your father and my father were different men but the same shameless person. I fought the enemy outside as he raised an enemy from within. So here I am, honouring my mother and listening to my father. I have come to fight an enemy. You. You have eaten enough. It is our time to eat. It is my time.

When we have cooked you, we will give your spine to the dogs. No man should eat a weak spine, or he, too, will stand for nothing. And what type of man is that? We will eat your brain and the rest of your body. But we will leave your head and keep it for anyone who may think that you have done great things for the people of this country. They will know that they were wrong.

We will enjoy your wife for you, but your son will know the same fate as you. We will leave all that you own for others who call themselves your relatives to fight for. We do not need it. We are the country.

Do you have any last requests?

~ Six ~

LIONS EAT MEAT

One lion eats a zebra, the other a gazelle. Both lions eat meat.

"I hate you! I hate you!" Even though they are not fully grown in mind, children somehow find ways to test the fragility of their parents' hearts. For a second, and just a second, Lucien's jaw locked, molar pressed on molar, grinding against breaking. His shoulders dropped and curled in, but he tightened back just as fast.

As he exhaled, he pointed to the ground right in front of him, *"Come here now!"*

Our child bowed his head and walked quickly to his father, who crouched to meet his eyes.

If this was four years ago, I would have jumped in, held Lucien's hand and stopped my boy from butting heads. Four years ago was before my mother held me down to my seat when I tried to stand up from our meal to play mediator during a verbal wrestle between the boys. I remember looking at her, the threat clear without the need for words, and her response being a continued firm hold of my hand.

She said, *"Tuula wansi. When you and I were like them, did you ever see your father step between us? If he is wrong, you will find time to tell him elsewhere. But to say to a father that he is wrong in front of your boy is not good for him. After all, Lucien is who he will become, just like you have become me."*

* * * * *

Eventually, the children fell asleep, and he poured a glass for himself. He rubbed his wrists before picking up the glass off the table with his right hand whilst his left thumb pressed against his left ring finger. It was a soother, like a mother rubbing her child's head. The grey in his hair had grown and spread, with most of the twists now grey and not enough black to cover it. When he sat down lost in thought, he would bite - almost chew - on the inside of his left cheek as he brushed his chin with knuckles. How time flies, and yet some things never change.

When our son was born, Lucien would not hold him until I had. Where he was from, the one who had carried the child was to speak life into the child through voice, touch, and spirit. Only when they were not present would the other do so first. Otherwise, it was like a stranger introducing one to their very own bed.

With our girls, he did not have to wait long to greet them, but our son's big head meant they had to put me to sleep and cut me open. Only the sound of our son's crying woke me up to see Lucien chewing his left cheek and rubbing his chin.

"Lucien. Lucien. You can hold him."

"But Eva, that's not what we agreed."

"How else will he stop crying, Lucien?" Lucien chewed his cheek some more, and then he began to hum. He was quiet at first, almost nervous, but with each hum, he grew confident, with

tears in his eyes. The hums reached our son's soul, and his rest-lessness subsided into a bout of sleep. As I began to fade back into my own, I wondered whether Lucien had more streaks of grey in his afro.

* * * * *

All of a sudden, the children started crying. His eyes closed, jaws locked, and then he exhaled.

"What's going on? Why are you guys crying?" He shouted into the hallway from his chair.

"He pinched me!!"

"Why did you pinch her?"

"Baba, I can't sleep!"

"Why?"

"Because I am not tired, Baba! Only old people like you get tired during the day!" Even though they are not fully grown in mind, children somehow find ways to test the fragility of their parents' hearts. For a second, and just a second, his jaw locked, molar pressed on molar, grinding against breaking. His shoulders dropped and curled in, but he tightened back just as fast.

As he exhaled, he pointed to the ground right in front of him, *"Jean-Jacques, come here now!"*

From the couch, I would watch the boys and smile. Here was our Edison, who had once hated everything about my Lucien, now carrying Jean-Jacques and humming them to sleep. Where he hid his grey in twists, Lucien had done in an afro. Where he poured orange juice, Lucien had poured white wine. The jaws still locked. The shoulders dropped and curled in. The insides of cheeks were chewed, and chins rubbed by knuckles. One lion eats a zebra, the other a gazelle. Both lions eat meat.

I whisper to Lucien, *"Do you see what I mean now?"*

~ Seven ~

PENALTY

And for five years, I could not
touch her.

Akili was smart and dangerous, but he died because he thought he was Solomon. The woman who killed him was a child when they first met. He had slaughtered her parents and taken her brother. As a woman, she had waited for her vengeance. And though many will never speak of her and what she did, her vengeance was our liberation. A way for many of us who left to come back home and for those who had stayed to be able to speak again.

What Marie and I had left behind was no longer here when we arrived. Where we had once planted a lemon tree for Marie was now just dead roots covered in cracked soil. The glass in all the windows had been smashed. Layers of cardboard covered the window length behind the red metal bars that used to hold the window glass I bought from Papa Mukusa.

The front door handle used to be a long metal one painted gold. Now, it was a hole with many copper wires plated together. They were the type of wires I had sent Marie to ask Felicien for when Marie's Shanga's husband's diarrhoea blocked the toilet from flushing. There was no way to ask them to leave after the two-week visit had turned into four months, but somehow, the diarrhoea pushed him to leave to wherever next he and Marie's Shanga would visit. It is surprising to learn what can make a man respond. Okocha would have stayed, and that is why I begged Marie to let us leave the morning after Akili took power.

Okocha could have died at least five times. The first time was right after he was tackled in the box. We had been playing together on this same field since we were children, using balls made of plastic bags, elastic bands, and ropes. We would play barefoot, with one team shirtless, to be able to tell the difference. The goalposts were bricks and stones from the chantiers that were never finished because the owner ran out of money. Politicians who had stolen, but their bellies had swallowed the dollars faster than the cement could be mounted and dried. Or some man had tried to build a home for his children to have a better life, but his small man salary had not budgeted for the tiny expenses "les honorables" and their assistants would ask of them. At first, their stubbornness would make them push forward, but soon, frustration would set in, and those who wanted to be defiant would eventually let go of the house, or life would let them go.

Okocha started by watching us play. When we finished school, I would pick him up from primary 1 along with Nzola-Nzabo. As we got to the field, Nzola-Nzabo would run ahead, up the steps, and through the wooden corrugated roof doors. Once he was in, Okocha would hold my bag as I threw my uniform in and changed into the shorts and t-shirt Mama had gotten from Mama Sylvain when Sylvain outgrew them. Playing football in uniform was guaranteed a beating from Mama and a night of studying whilst kneeling when Baba arrived. Mama would still be mad about dirty clothes, but, unlike the school uniform, she would wash these and deliver no beating.

Okocha would sit on the small hill on the side. We had found an empty bag once used for rice and placed two stones to hold it down. Okocha could not get dirty, or esle we would both collect beatings when Mama came from the market. We would play until the bells of the cathedral rang for evening mass with Pere Jean-Pierre. The bells were not just a way of telling time but also to remind all the women who would go for evening mass that the mass had started. The men who could not drink at home would have two hours to drink as fast as possible and then chew on garlic and onions to cover their breath. It was also when the market closed for all those with children. Those who stayed would try their last chance at selling to men who had angered their wives the night before or men who lived alone and had decided to cook something beyond rice and sugar. Those who were really selling food would leave the market by the end of the first evening mass. Any other person selling in the market after that was not selling fruit- no fruit became ripe in darkness.

Okocha used to shout commands like a coach on the sidelines but for both teams. He would tell people to defend, cross the ball, run, call out fouls and offside. The only time he was not shouting was when running after the ball to make sure it did not go down into the drain that led to the lake. He annoyed everyone on the pitch so much that Patrick pulled him from the sideline by the time he turned six years old and told him to do all the things he used to like shouting about. He was a six year old playing with nine to twelve year olds. For the first two months, Okocha was pushed and tackled by everyone. There was almost no day he did not have grazes and wounds on his legs and arms. But he kept coming back even when Patrick tried to break his leg. When we were not studying, working for Mama, at church, or school, Okocha would play with the football he had begged me to make him. He started running as fast as the older boys, but because he was smaller, many other boys did not see him until it was too late. The only balls Okocha did not win were the ones in the air, but he always tried to reach for them. Somehow, the nine to twelve year olds on the field would begin to listen to petit Jean-Pi, which made it easier for me as I never had to call out fouls or aggressive players on the field.

Petit Jean-Pi soon became Jean-Pi on terrain de Deuxième Zone. Mama had to sweat more at the market and fight for her customers to not buy her food and vegetables at low prices. She looked for women who came to the market wearing gold brace-lets and make-up. Those who had come to the market as if it were a wedding. Or the ones who would squeeze their whole body so they would not have to step into the mud and the market's waters. They were ba mamans Jaune and ba mamans Tala Kiato, who would speak to Mama without looking at her and behula as if she was vomit or the poopoo that had been smelling. Mama would bow her head, where a bag of tomato was 1 franc Con-golais, Mama would sell It to her for 3 franc Congolais. But she would start at 5 francs Congolais so the woman could feel like she had bargained for a good deal. They did not know they had lost the moment they walked into the market.

Sometimes, Mama had to be careful with the Mamans Jaune. Some of them were actually women who had grown up in or near the market and then stumbled upon a man who used mil franc congolais as a pillow. Mama would find those ones because they would be bizarre. They would wear gold bracelets but no earrings. Or wear kikwembes that looked high-quality but were the waka waka kind. People who had come into money and wanted to show it. Mama would say they were like the gold bracelets Papa Gregoire sold that were bronze. If it wasn't in what they wore, it was their tongue that revealed them.

They would start in French, *"Combien pour les tomatoes?"* And then all other tongues would slip in as she refused the price, *"Nanga la. Hapana!"* before she realised what she had done and quickly found the words in French again.

This was how Mama made enough food for Baba and her two mushamuka as our appetites grew. With football, every morning and after school, Jean-Pi and I ate four boules of fufu each per meal and Baba ate two - sometimes three. Mama would eat one, and sometimes she would not eat at all because she was praying for her children to finish secondary school and university, then get good jobs in Sese's government and marry good women. We laughed at Mama when she would say this. Marriage and working for Sese's government were not in our minds.

When Okocha entered secondary school, he and I used to go play with Tornado, Tanke, and the Beke Dawa team when they were not training for a match. They played a different kind of football to the one Okocha, and I played when we were younger. It used to feel like playing football and boxing at the same time because of the way they pushed and tackled. It was bad enough that Okocha and I would find ourselves limping back home after the game. But the Beke Dawa team had learned how to be aggressive enough to hurt the other players but not so much for them to bleed or the referee to be sure it was a foul. These men had bones. Okocha and I used to avoid playing against people like Tanke. Players would run into Tanke or push him, and they would feel the pain. These men ate bugali Burma, and there were very few people who were more dangerous than that. So we adapted to their game, waking up even earlier for pompano and running. On the field, I started pushing and tackling, while Okocha became nimble and would dance over tackles and out of the way of a defender aiming to push him to the ground. While Tornado and Tanke had strength, Okocha had speed and would tire them out running back and forth. His speed and dancing tactic earned him the names Danseur and Flash. Meanwhile, I played between Tanke and Tornado, shouting out when the formation needed to change and about the weaknesses of each player. I became Cervo for all my match tactics. Les garçons de Mushagalusa dominated the field. I would hold defence with Tornado and Tanke while finding different ways to feed the ball to Flash so he could dance into a goal. We played like this when we joined Tornado and Tanke as part of the Beke Dawa official team.

Even though Okocha was only 14 years old at the time, Coach Gilbert was so impressed by him that he lied to other teams that he was 18. In the year we played together for Beke Dawa, Okocha scored 35 goals, and we only lost one game through penalties. We thought Papa and Mama never watched us play because they would not want to hear anything about football. They did not work for their children to be vagabonds- kicking a football and drinking beer. We didn't drink, even when we won, we never followed the others into any nganda. Even when Tornado and Tanke almost convinced us that we would not touch any alcohol, we still went home. They promised to buy us as many bottles of Coca as we wanted. Still, Okocha had a French exam in the morning, and if he failed, Papa would definitely ban us from even thinking about football.

In September, after a year of playing with Beke Dawa, Papa sent me to Lushi to study at UniLu. He thought being away from Beke Dawa would ensure I would finish school and not play football. One son safe from football, he now had to wait three more years before he could also send Okocha away. I chose to study law at Unilu after Papa Marc had told me and Baba about how his son Prince had studied law and immediately got a job from Sese to work in an embassy in Senegal. Land of people like Ousmane Sembene. If I worked hard enough, Prince would refer me to the office in Abidjan. Papa Marc said that the Ivorians were just like the Congolese people. If we were to ever go, we would think that they were our cousins. Papa Marc had visited Abidjan with Prince when they had gone to buy wedding clothes for Prince's sister Jeanette. They had this food like rice but ate it like a bugali called Attieke. Papa Marc had explained that it was said as acheke but spelt as Attieke.

Law was difficult. When many boys in my block would write letters to different women, those of us in law slept in the libraries or with our books on our beds. It was only those in geology that used to wake up before us. There was almost no time to play football except for Saturday early morning before bathing and walking around town to visit Baba Tina, Mama Lily, or Tonton Delvo. We would alternate who we would visit, so we would see each family after every two weeks. With the tontons and papas, we would talk about Sese's work and the houses he was building; with the mamas, we would talk about families, and they would ask us about when we would bring them their daughters-in-law. We would come around 12, right as the onions were frying in the oil but before the hot water was boiling for bugali and we would find ways to continue the conversation until we smelled the food was fully ready. Usually, it was when there was no more banging of the mwiko on the pots. At that point we would stand up and start to say our farewells, only to be told to sit down and join them for a meal. We would eat and eat until our stomachs pressed our belts. When we were full, the children would run from the kitchen to each one of us and give us a plastic bag of food that was left over. That would be dinner for Monday and Tuesday. We would sit for another hour with them before making our way to Jardin.

We would meet others that we had split away from when dividing ourselves into houses we would go to eat at. Students would be spread around Jardin, and those with a cherie would force all their friends to walk with all her friends. In the daytime, being alone with a woman who wasn't a wife would bring more problems than one needed. Some men would walk with one woman and her friend during the day, and at night they would eat from another woman. We knew through

whispers and the nights when boys would talk about their esca-
pades and heartbreaks that the night was where many things
happened. Soeur Nancy, who would walk and go to church with
frère Henri- who planned to marry her when he finished in a
year, became Da Nana, who would make men capable of being
her father and promise their children's school fees to her. Meanwhile, Theo used to find women whose husbands would travel
for work for two to three weeks and provide them comfort. The
women told their husbands he was the son of their uncle who
had died tragically in the village, and the husbands would send
him on errands and entrust his family to Theo.

The end of the month was a dangerous time. We would get
200 francs, and some would drink half of it before morning the
next day. I would send some to Baba and Mama, then a bit more
to Okocha. The rest I used to buy food, transport, and gifts for
Ciza to add to the letters I would send her with someone going
home. At the end of the year, all of us who had received scholarships for passing secondary school, with more than 60%, were
given money to travel home.

At home, petit Jean-Pi had grown to be as tall as me. In his joy of
becoming more of a man, he kept a moustache and grew his hair
to Lumumba's length. A choice that became a point of discussion
almost every day with Mama and for which shortened Baba's patience even more. When I arrived, Mama had prepared food for
a whole village with wali, kihembe, nyama ya mbuzi, mashanza,
bugali, pondu, and makemba. She had asked Mama Nzola
to come along with Baba Nzola and Nzola-Nzabo, who now wore
glasses from reading too much math and chemistry. He still
did not talk much, but he paid more attention than before. He
and Okocha were in the same class, but he asked a lot more

questions about university every chance he was able to get me alone. Okocha had decided he would do geology and the rest would figure itself out because he already had enough of school straining his football plans. During exams he had been put on the bench and only played two games, which was really a punishment for Okocha. He had gotten used to starting and playing the full 90-minutes of a match. When exams ended and the holidays began, Mama would only see Okocha twice in the day - once in the morning as he carried Mama's things to the market, and the second at dinner right before he went to sleep. Baba would try as much as he could to fight against all the football, but when Okocha would come among the top five - the first always being Nzola - there was almost nothing he could say. We all sat and ate the meal Mama had prepared after Baba had asked Baba Nzola to pray.

On the Saturday of my return, Okocha woke me before the sun rose. He made us jog up the hill towards Zone Industrielle, only to run some more as we played alongside Tanque, Tornado, and men who worked in the factories. Okocha had started playing with them a few months ago because he found it too easy to play against the men at Terrain du Deuxieme Zone. They were faster, stronger, and much rougher. One of the players, Rocky, had warned me that they played football for men, not children. They would tackle with their whole body, and no fouls would be given unless blood was seen or bones were broken. Having played with them before, Okocha, Tanque, and Tornado had learned how to push back and avoid tackles aimed for the ankles. I was not so lucky. By the end of the game, I could only step on my right foot if I did not place my heel on the ground. The match ended at a draw only because people had started to wake up for exercise and street cleaning. We had done our own exercise, but Governor Balemba had made it so that everyone above the age of five who could walk was required to clean their neighbourhoods.

Children ran around pulling plastic and rubbish from drains or sides of streets and putting them together in one corner. The mamas would sweep away the dust on the ground in a line as their kifagio caught what the mama in front of them missed. Mothers with babies would tie them onto their backs as they did this, and not a sound would be made from them throughout it. All the young women and girls would scrub the walls using a bucket, a yellow jerrycan, brushes, and cloth rags. Men carried the rubbish away and moved objects out of the way for sweeping and wall scrubbing. We also carried jerrycans for our homes from the wells or taps nearby. I would start by helping Mama before finding a way to carry rubbish in the direction of where Ciza was working. The cleaning became an opportunity to talk with her, Cito and Cikuru. Okocha would try and distract Mum as I worked with them. Since the only boy in Ciza's family was 12 year old Bruno, it was also easy to work with them. I would carry their jerrycans and drop them in front of Mama Nyabadeux - making sure to greet her briefly before leaving. Ciza's family had to know I was serious about their daughter. Even though Mama knew this too, she would not ask about Ciza but whether I had passed her greetings to Mama Nyabadeux.

In the month that I was there, Okocha played a match in the stadium every week and scored, but at the end of the game, he returned home with me. He still feared Baba's rage. He would do the same during the week when he played at Terrain du Deuxième Zone, or Zone Industrielle. This remained the same the next year when I returned, except when we walked home, we would escort Emmanuella and her two sisters, who had brought their brother, Jerry, to watch Beke Dawa play. In truth, Jerry could go by himself but - like Ciza and I - they used the 15 minutes of walking and the football match as camouflage for them to be able to spend time together and talk to each other.

Okocha started to drink when I returned to UniLu. I found out through Mama, who had told Tonton Delvo's sister to tell me when she visited Tonton Delvo for six months. At the end of the month, I called Francis twice. Once, I told him to tell Okocha to be by the phone at 4pm, and the second time I called, Okocha picked up the phone. He did not speak about football. He was angry. He spoke of being a man and Mama thinking he was still a child. I stopped him before he cursed our mother; I did not want him or me to be cursed. Okocha had the beard of a man and kicked the ball with boys who considered themselves men, but his heart was still a child's. I asked after Emmanuella, and there was nothing good to say. He kept repeating how she would regret leaving him when he was playing football all over the world. Then she would see whether an engineer was better than a footballer. The things men and boys will do when they are freshly in love, women will never understand.

I told him of Janvier, a striker at UniLu who was about to graduate and was a better footballer than drunk Jean-Pi. And Primus left Okocha immediately. His words became clear as he asked how many goals had Janvier scored. I lied and said he had 60 goals, and Okocha lied and said he had scored 67, and in the next game, he would score four goals. I laughed and told him how Janvier knew how to dance with the ball and score beautiful goals. Okocha told me to ask Tanque and Tornado how he played in the last games. Kuchenga ba grand was his profession; he could do it in his sleep. We talked a bit more, but my time on the telephone finished.

It was a month before I called again to speak to Mama. They still could not get their Jean-Pi to be the son they knew. There comes a time when children become parents, and parents become children, and with Jean-Pi's behaviour, Mama and Papa no longer had the strength to raise their child. When Mama and I had finished talking, we agreed that Okocha would spend his Easter holiday with me in UniLu. It was now up to Mama to convince Papa, and she would as soon as she mentioned that he would not be the one paying for Okocha's trip.

His hair was not combed, and his beard, which he used to spend time shaving properly, was now patches on his face like the patches of weed by the drainage and sewage system by Stade de Douze. This would change before the end of the night and not because of them. The first thing he wanted to do was find Janvier and see him train, but when he entered the room, Blaise, Ntabo, and Bahati were waiting for him. The four of us shared a room together in Block Neuf. Okocha did not know that Block neuf was Block de Jeune-Homme. We kept our hairs short or, at most, well combed. A moustache was allowed, but a beard was not. Shorts were only acceptable in the block or when playing sports; otherwise, every jeune homme was expected to wear black shoes, well-ironed trousers, a shirt tucked into a belt, and a jacket. Sleeves could only be folded on a hot day, at the very end of the day when there were no more classes, or a Saturday evening. Watches had to be worn on the left hand. Hands had to be lotioned. Only black, baby blue, or grey plain socks could be worn underneath the trousers and black shoes. And these shoes could only be shoes that Wazabanga himself could wear. Any woman or elder was never to walk on the side closest to the road. We were never to be seen drunk. If another jeune-homme saw their brother not following Les Accord de Jeune Hommes, they would tell Capitaine of this infraction. A correction would follow, maybe not immediately, maybe at the end of the day, or the following week when even the jeune homme who told Capitaine would forget.

For me, it was at four in the morning. Capitaine came with a bucket of cold water and poured it slowly across my bed. I woke up angry and ready to fight Bahati, only to see Capitaine and four other jeune hommes standing over me. I was told to run to heaven. I lay with my back on the ground and pushed my legs to run until Capitaine said I could stop. With all the sweat, they carried me to stand right outside the block. Capitaine poured a few drops of water and told me to show him how I used to swim when I was a child. They left me alone when it was close to six, when the sky was beginning to show some blue in it. Too late for me to sleep again, but too early to do anything after washing off the soil from the swim. Ntabo later told me that I had been seen without a watch on my left hand.

For Okocha, his correction was his welcome. Bahati greeted him first and explained the room. He didn't get far before Blaise interrupted to introduce himself and ask if Okocha had packed his football clothes. Ntabo stopped him before he could start to tease Okocha by reminding him that Okocha was here to learn about the importance of school and how to be a proper man. Ntabo jumped off his bed and stood right in front of Okocha. They were about the same height, but Okocha somehow had to look up as they shook hands. And there was no escape once

Okocha's right hand met Ntabo's. Ntabo held Okocha's hand in place as Bahati and Blaise stood by either shoulder and lifted him by his shorts into the chair near the wall opposite the door. Blaise called for Capitaine. Okocha fought, wiggled, and stretched like Mimi did when her mother was forcing her to eat. But all three jeune hommes held on. Okocha looked towards me and could not find my eyes. He needed to learn, and this was a way he would never forget. I also was not in the mood to swim again. When Okocha left the room to meet Janvier, he wore a white shirt, black trousers, black socks, black shoes padded with toilet paper, and a black tie. He complained of the heat, and I handed him a handkerchief to wipe sweat off his bald head and bare cheeks.

Okocha spent eight days at UniLu during Easter. I was with him on the first day he arrived. When we passed through town, he met all the jeune hommes, including Janvier, saw the whole campus, and Tonton Delvo. The next time I spent an entire day with Okocha was on Sunday. We woke up for church and walked with all the jeune hommes. Then, those whom Tonton Delvo had adopted made their way to his house. We prayed, ate, laughed, drank, ate some more and then excused ourselves earlier than usual. Okocha had to find a way to pack the pineapples, clothes, and decorations Mama had told him to buy. On Monday morning ten jeune hommes escorted us to Okocha's bus. They all had to make sure that Blockonz did not fall whilst wearing his new white shirt, black trousers, and black shoes.

Jean-Pi had slept on the outside of the bed and I slept on the inside, like we used to do when Shaga, Mugisho, Frederic, Cirhula, and Bienfait would spend Bonane with us. At four-thirty in the morning, Janvier would knock twice, and Okocha would slide out of bed. He would return an hour later, change into other shorts, quickly wash the shorts and t-shirt, hang them on the line as I had shown him, then rinse out the bucket to use again to bathe. When I would wake up at six, Okocha would be in the hallway with other jeune homme. There was no need to keep an eye on him. The jeune hommes would find different times to tell me about what Okocha had been doing.

On his second day, Jean-Pi went with Ntabo to a debate, then was grabbed by Blaise for bible study, only to be taken to a bar by Bahati that night. I did not wait for them to return. It was only at four thirty when Janvier came to knock on the door that we all woke up to find Jean-Pi was not in the room. Bahati mumbled he had left him, walking towards Block Onze to use the bathroom. Block Onze was a little bush where we went for anything longer than one minute. So we all put on our mapapas and went there first. When we arrived, we found Jean-Pi lying on the ground five steps away from Block One. His belt unbuckled, button undone, zip halfway, and his beige pants brown from where he had urinated on himself. Ntabo slapped him four times as if Okocha were one of his seven brothers. Okocha stretched his hand and turned from sleeping on his side to his stomach, brushing off Blaise's slaps in the process. Some of the jeune hommes started to laugh and more laugh when Blaise landed the full weight of his palm on Okocha's face. Kofi! Okocha found himself standing before he could even think. Capitaine looked at the rest of the jeune hommes, and they all stopped laughing - at least on the outside. We returned to our block in silence. When Okocha went to bathe, Capitaine came in to ask that he meet him after he was finished.

Capitaine made Okocha scrubs every tile that could be stepped on with a toothbrush. And he made him sing *"pombe siwezi, siko mulevi"* until he finished. Capitaine then took him on a walk around campus, and that was the last time Okocha ever touched a beer. Claude saw him first when he came back and started clapping. Other jeune hommes joined him as Charles started singing a song about La Garde de Block Onze. And that's how the jeune hommes forgot Jean-Pi's name. Garde de Block Onze then became Garde, or Blocking. Eventually it became Blockonz as the jeune hommes prayed, shook his hand, and wished him a safe journey as he entered the bus. We stood there for another thirty minutes talking while waiting for Blockonz's bus to take off. All of us knew never to turn our back to travellers, so we only made our way back to campus once we could no longer see Blockonz's head.

Two weeks after Okocha left, all the jeune homme went to a concert. It was the same as going to church on an easter or New Years. Everyone wore their best shoes. Capitaine brought out les crocodiles; others had their serpent. Trousers were ironed until there was no more charcoal for it. One either wore an Abacost or a suit, but more of us wore an Abacost. Rumba, Kwassa kwassa, salsa, mutuashi, jazz and anything else, the jeune homme would not leave the dance floor. Some danced with one woman the whole night and everyone understood she was madam. Others danced with many women through the night to find their own madam. Then there were some who danced with a few women but not to too many songs. These were the snipers of the group. They would leave there with a madam, but no one would know until years later when they were married. I danced with many women but never coller-serrer to let them know all that there would be between us was this dance. When the night got darker and those with sense became fewer, I left. No woman here could take Ciza's place, and I was not interested to find out.

We walked to the concert as a group of jeune hommes and stayed close to each other for the first hour. Blaise, Bahati, Ntabo, and I showed each other dances we had yet to show each other in the room. One would start, then another would add without ever forcing or planning. We would all laugh every time Blaise would lead, because he always had danced funny dances seriously. Ntabo's dance was the dance of Monsieur l'Honorable. Bahati was the true dancer. Sometimes we had to slow him down because his dances were "za kuvunja migulu". Some jeune hommes left before I did, but those who were there when I was ready to leave were sedans. I let Ntabo know I was leaving, and he nodded to show that he would tell the others. At this time, taking a taxi would have been expensive because there was no one to share it with. I took a motto instead, and we zigzagged through the small traffic outside the concert.

I woke up the next morning with my left leg on fire. Ntabo was in a chair reading some book by Rousseau, Molier or this other African intellectual he had been speaking about - Fanane or something. When he realised I was awake, he looked at his watch and told me I should have slept a little long so Blaise and Bahati would owe him money. How long had I been asleep for? Ntabo explained that I had been asleep since the accident. The doctors in the hospital had said it was the body's response to shock, but I was lucky only the side of my left leg had been burned by the moto's engine. It began to make sense why the lights were on and felt brighter. It was another three weeks in the hospital before I could leave.

Blaise, Ntabo, and Bahati took turns to drop off notes that Gauthier had taken for me, as I learned to walk again. Capitaine and other jeune hommes also passed by a few times to see how I was progressing. When Capitaine came to visit, he forced me to walk. Ntabo had to tell Tonton Delvo about the accident on the second Sunday they visited him without me. The next day, Tonton Delvo was by my bedside lecturing me about telling these things to parents, while his wife continued to pray the rosary in tears. I asked Tonton Delvo not to tell my mother, and he nodded but a quick glance at his wife, Mama Sebastian, told me that they knew already.

It was my first time almost facing death, but Okocha's only came many years later. After he had started at UniLu and even after I graduated. Even with his mischief and all his travelling for football and etudes du terrain for geology, he never had a scare. Blockonz became Capitaine, and got his redemption waking younger jeune hommes the same way our Capitaine and then Ntabo - who became Capitaine in our last year - had done. Okocha managed to escape Ciza's anger when he arrived late to our wedding because he had been playing football.

He never got malaria when he would travel for work to monitor the progress of the mines. Four of his friends had died on site. Okocha would laugh and say it was because they never ate soil as children. With him travelling to mines and returning every three months, Okocha could not play football with one team long enough to be scouted for the national team. But every time he came back to Beke, he would join the training matches and play socially with the team I coached - Zone Deux. Ciza had agreed to let me coach football as long as I didn't play. She had seen my left leg swell too many times and did not understand why I could not just focus on the government job, rebuilding our parents' home, our own home, and Malaika. She stopped speaking about it because we finished building our house or because she was tired of talking to a stubborn husband.

Okocha through UniLu and even whilst at the mines met many women. Before he was Capitaine, but after Blockonz, many had called him a Sniper Dangereux at UniLu. But none of the women ever lasted and Mama kept asking if he was winging for her to die to give her grandkids. And she almost did when we left her.

Okocha got tackled in the box and everyone called for a penalty. Okocha placed the ball and Junior, Kachinja's son, started dancing around the goal like the gardiens did on tv. Okocha took four steps back. Many people had seen him do the same thing in other matches for free kicks, and had called him Okocha because his free kicks reminded them of Okocha's free kick against Algeria. He dropped his hand, but right then, a gun went off, then another. I did not wait for a third. I ran onto the pitch, grabbed Okocha's hand and ran. We heard trucks behind us but did not stop running. Okocha ran ahead of me, and if it was not for the guns still ringing, my leg would have stopped me.

We ran through Deuxième Zone, down the hill by Lycée, and across the field in front of Hopital Generale. We could still hear the trucks. Okocha turned to run to the right but I pulled him back just as the first truck came flying by. It knocked a boy wearing navy blue trousers and a white shirt. He was probably in secondary. The truck did not stop, and neither did the seven others. We turned left, squeezed in between two houses, took a right and made it to the lake. There was no one around by the water, and all doors were locked. We could hear muffled screams when we knocked, begging for someone to open.

I pulled Okocha from a door and told him to grab a bunch of nets and we jumped into a pirogue. We lay flat and covered ourselves with the nets smelling of fish until we felt the town calm down six hours later. We crawled out of the pirogue and slowly walked back. We would hide behind houses or trees until we were sure the road was clear to cross. Outside Hopital General, we saw the secondary schoolboy's body with red where his head was supposed to be, and his legs flattened. We passed the body. Okocha kept looking back at it. He wanted to do something, but he also wanted to make sure Mama and Baba were safe. We had left them with Ciza, Malaika, and Jacques. We knocked on the door. No one responded. We pushed the door until it opened just a bit and a mpanga came swinging through, just missing my shoulder. Baba had been by the door with his mpanga. He had locked the door and put a table right on it. Mama held Malaika, and Ciza held Jacques as they squeezed themselves under the table.

We helped Baba move the table back onto the door and for three days we all slept near the table with Mama, Ciza, Malaika, and Jacques right underneath it. Baba, Jean-Pi, and I changed between watching the door, watching the women and the children, and listening to the radio. Mama was the only one that ever went through the door. We had tried to stop her, but she asked us how we expected to eat. We offered to go, but Mama explained that we, her sons, were too young and the army could take us. As for Baba, he simply did not know how to bargain for good prices and food. She was an old woman, none of the young boys would give her trouble. If they did, she would go naked and turn them mad.

General Akili had put a couvre-feu in place for 7pm, and even if he had not, the fear of him and his men did. Nine days after the trucks first came through Deuxième Zone, a truck came into Zone Deux, and one of Akili's men announced that all boys who were 15 and older were to register for army training. Also, all men not yet married were to make themselves useful and join the army. We all looked at Jean-Pi. Mama started crying and telling Jean-Pi that he should have listened to her instead of hoping ata achanisha Emmanuelle and Nzabo. Now, he would have to join the army. We did not speak after the announcement except for Jacques crying and Malaika singing to herself.

At night, I lay by Ciza and we spoke about Okocha. We had seen others leave their homes with all they could carry. Paulin had said that people were going to try and make a new home in Tanzania, Kenya, or Uganda. Ciza knew we needed to leave, but she did not know if our children would handle the journey. I promised her that they would. She accepted and we agreed to tell Baba and Mama in the morning. The morning came, Baba refused to go and told us he would not leave his home that he had fought for. These boys would eventually get tired. He told us to leave him. And Mama refused to leave her husband. That same morning, I ran home and gathered all that I could from what Ciza had told me, then returned to meet Ciza, Okocha, and the children. She had Jacques on her back and placed a kikwembe full of our things on her head. Okocha carried more of the stuff on his back and head as I balanced Malaika on my back and the last of the things on my head. Baba and Mama gave us their baraka, placing the sign of the cross on our forehead and slapping our cheeks gently. We did the same to them.

Baba kissed Malaika's forehead, and Malaika hugged her tates. Jacques was asleep, but both his tates placed their hands on his head. Mama then looked at Ciza and, in front of all of us, told her that she was now the mother. Her strength was what would keep the family together - akaze. Then she reached into her breast and removed a scarf full of money. She passed this to Ciza, we prayed, and then we left. It was not hard to know where to go, even after six days of Akili, there were long lines of people leaving the town, and we followed it.

As we crossed the border, we came across a woman managing four children by herself. An older boy was carrying things on his head and his younger brother, the second youngest, on his back. The youngest was on the woman's back. She was a small girl wearing small gold earrings. The second oldest was also a girl. She wore the same gold earrings as her sister and a copper bracelet. She carried a bag that was almost the same size as her five-year-old self. We would have walked past them if Ciza had not told Okocha that the woman was pregnant. He made us stop and introduce ourselves to her. She greeted us respectfully but refused to give us her name or her children's names. Okocha tried to ask the second oldest for her name, but her mother's litcho made her quiet immediately. Okocha said he would call her Mama Batoto and that she did not need to talk, but since she was pregnant, she would give him the things she was carrying on her head. Mama Batoto was shocked that Okocha knew she was pregnant, and her oldest son did not hide his anger at hearing it, even if he did not say anything. I got to see how Okocha earned the name Sniper Dangereux.

His gentleman charm managed to convince Mama Batoto to add her things to what he was already carrying.

We made it to Kampala. This was three years after we had left Mama and Baba. Okocha had learned Mama Batoto's name through her daughter Christelle. Children will tell the truth where adults cannot. We spent the first year moving through Rwanda. We passed through Gisenyi. Okocha and I worked anywhere to make enough money to feed the twelve of us. Mama Batoto's first son would join us when he could, but we forced him to stay in school. We smashed stones for roads, built homes, carried things in town and the market for people, and cleaned toilets. Mama Batoto gave birth to Celine, and we became thirteen. Okocha and I could not get jobs that paid well, and the children were not being taught well at school. They would cry because other teachers called them poor or told them they smelled and were stupid. The truth was the community did not like many of us who had come to seek refuge in their town.

We moved again to a town outside Kigali. All thirteen of us lived in two houses that had one bedroom each. Even though Okocha and Mama Batoto had become friends, Okocha slept in our house. He explained that Mama Batoto was not ready for the presence of another man in her life. I tried to ask more, but Ciza - knowing something I did not - held my hand to stop me. This town also had many people who had run away from Beke. Some were young men who had run away from joining Akili's army. Unable to get the jobs they wanted, some of them became vagabonds. Some others formed gangs that robbed and taxed vulnerable people. One day, they decided they would try to rob Mama Batoto of her money and her womanhood. I had taken Ciza, Malaika, and Jacques to a field to spend some time with my children. Okocha, knowing this, decided to stay behind and rest. This was the second time he almost died.

He heard three men in Mama Batoto's house shouting. He took his hammer and ran into her house. Three men stood over her and four of her children. Her oldest son had gotten some work that afternoon and was not among her children. Okocha struck the first one over the head with his hammer and the second in the knees, but he was slow in hitting the third man, and the man stabbed Okocha's left shoulder. The man grabbed his friend bleeding on the ground and ran away with the third man limping out with his hammered knee. Mama Batoto carried Okocha to the hospital but told her thirdborn, her second son, to stay so that he could tell us where they had gone. We left town at the end of the month. This time by bus for Kabale.

In Kabale, we became twelve. Our daughter, Malaika, died. Doctors had said she had gotten pneumonia from the cold mornings of Kabale. We had thought it was a bad fever and cough. We gave all the types of tea we could think of. Gave her drugs from the pharmacy. Malaika did not get better. We took her to the hospital when she could barely open her eyes. Malaika died on a Wednesday and we buried her on a Thursday in a graveyard not too far from Ainembabazi Primary School. Ciza never spoke about Malaika, and for five years, I could not touch her - even when I woke up to her crying and screaming Malaika's name in her dreams.

Ciza became Marie. It was easier for her to use Marie so the Ugandans would not ask her about where she was from every time she said her name. She stayed as Marie five years later when her brothers Cito and Cikuru passed within six months of each other. Ciza was too painful a name after that. We returned to Beke the year after. Mama Batoto had told me going home would save my wife. So, we left. Marie, Jacques and I. Okocha stayed in Kampala. He now managed three petrol stations and a truck driver system for imports and exports. He was beginning to buy land and property. We had bought one house together and rented it. The money from it was what we sent to Baba and Mama.

It was two years after we left that Okocha almost died a third time. He had just returned to Kampala after coming to Beke for Baba's funeral. He met his niece Jessica, who somehow managed to sleep in Mama Batoto's arms better than her Ba Muloko Jean-Pi. When he returned to Kampala, he went with Mama. We had agreed Mama would spend six months with him and Mama Batoto. On his way back from work one evening, Okocha's car was shot at. He had been financing a young politician running for office, and he had built a school that began to outperform the top school in the neighbourhood. His business, his involvement in the background of politics, and his success with the community had angered many people. And among the church, politicians, and business tyrants, someone had sent people to kill him. They shot at the driver's seat five times, and the sixth bullet tore through the door of the passenger seat behind the driver and into Okocha's right thigh.

Okocha had asked Ssebaganja to drive him through the night because he was too tired and could not stand the "cent-metre" other cars had on when driving on the road. Ssebaganja's body had swallowed the bullets meant for Okocha. And Okocha, in guilt, paid for all five of Ssebaganje's children's school fees all the way through to their first university degrees. When things became difficult and dangerous in Kampala, Okocha sent Mama Batoto to Kenya to buy property. They bought homes in Kisumu, Naivasha, South C, Ngong, and even Lavington. That way if they ever tried to block his money in Uganda, the houses in Kenya would still provide.

Jean-Pi was the person for everything. If one needed a visa, he had a contact. Jean-Pi had a contact if one needed a license, a construction tool, or an affordable hospital. He had a contact for Sudhir and even for the President. The three years we had done leaving Beke for Kampala had made Okocha someone who could do anything and everything once it was shown to him.

And in a situation like this, where a mother could no longer take care of her child, Okocha would know what to do. Losing a child is hard to recover from, and no one ever fully recovers. Marie cannot find more than two sentences every time Jessica asks about Malaika. And she was stuck in that silence for five years. Those were five years this child did not have to lose, and her mother would not be able to save herself from losing a second child.

"Cervo! Is that you? Or is this Jacques?
"Jean-Paul, it's me."
"Ahh, Baba Jacques. You are calling me by my name. Uko sawa?"
"Yes, niko sawa."
"And my sister?"
"She and the children are doing well."
"So what is the problem, Baba Jacques? You have not called me by name since Lionel was born."
"I need to ask you to do something for me, Jean-Paul."

~ Eight ~

MAMA SAMUEL

Apparently, we, young
people, think we are the only
ones who are smart.

Hi Tate Majina,

I reached safely, but I don't have good news about the letter you gave me.

I cannot find Baba's father. I had asked around until I came across an elderly woman, Mama Samuel, who told me she used to sell beer to Baba's father and knew him well. I didn't tell her who I was, just like you told me, but told her I had been given something to give him.

She did that thing that you and Ba Mudogo Lionel do. The one where you rub your ear very fast, and your throat clicks loudly. But hers is much quieter than Baba's, almost like yours, but then she coughs. She tried to ask me whose daughter I was, and I told her that I was not from here but from the east, visiting for work. She looked me up and down, and when she saw that I would not leave her without more information about Baba's father, she offered me a seat. She no longer sells beer but cement. Apparently, some woman had come into her bar and cursed her for their husband's death. That she had decided to rob all women of their husbands since she did not have any; only a woman with an evil heart would see families being destroyed and continue to make money from it. No one had ever spoken to her like that in all her life and to disgrace her husband's name. A man who loved her and her children with all his heart that he built them a house fit for a mwamikaze. If not for her in-laws, who came and took everything in his name, she would never have been found selling beer to other men. But that beer fed her child, put them through school, and even had the very same in-laws begging her for help when there was no more of her husband's money and land to eat. If she had not, another woman would have, because men and their beer in this town had a stronger bond than any husband and wife. But she saw the woman's eyes and remembered her own. The very next day, she started selling bags of cement on the side. It has now been two years and she has three stores. At her age Tate Majina! She's even older than you.

But by then, Baba's father was gone. I asked her if she knew where he had gone. If it was still in the neighbourhood or if he had moved to another town. I remember you once told me that Baba's father was like your Baba and had sworn never to leave the country.

Tate Majina, I hope you are sitting.

Baba's father married another woman less than a month after you left. Well, he didn't marry her until three years later, but a woman and man living in the same house and having children is what husband and wife do. She said that, and I thought of how you had told me otherwise. They had 7 children together, including twins. Mama Samuel was never sure what Baba's father was doing for work, but he had always managed to find enough for at least two bottles every day. She never asked.

There is no other way to say this Tate Majina. Baba's father and his family, along with the family of Mama Kaka, died 10 years ago in a fire. I could not believe it at first, but Mama Samuel closed her shop and walked me down to the place. The building is still there. A lot of it was blackened by the kerosene of the fire but abandoned with no windows, doors or people. There was a lot of grass, but it was not too long because an uncle who lived further down did not want any snakes.

I asked Mama Samuel why nothing had been done to the place after the fire. But she laughed. No one wants anything to do with where people have died. She said it would be another four years before someone tried to buy this land. In the meantime, it will stay as it is. I thought of it becoming a graveyard, but Mama Samuel rebuked it. It would spoil her business because then people would really believe that she was a witch.

When we got back to Mama Samuel's shop, she asked me if I had seen the room facing towards the lake. I nodded. I had spent nearly an hour there with Mama Samuel, walking around the outside and taking photos of as much as I could. Apparently, that was where Baba's father slept with his wife. But on the day of the fire, they found all the children in one room. Baba's father's wife had been found on the floor by her bed. Burnt worse than ripe plantain left in the oil for too long. Baba's father had been found by the door leading to the lounge. Some say that he had collapsed coming back from playing muchuba with Baba Kaka - too drunk to make it to his wife in the room. Some said he was on his way to making an eighth child with his wife. Mama Samuel says that Baba's father had actually left his wife and was trying to escape the fire.

Mama Samuel was about to offer me another Fanta and tell me more, but it was getting dark and I wanted to take a moto back to my hotel.

As I left, she told me that she was glad Da Lolo left him. She said Da Lolo was a good woman with a kind heart and a sharp brain. That Baba's father was a good man, but he was broken and that Da Lolo would have never gone far with him. Mama Samuel said Da Lolo would not have lived long. She then smiled and said I should greet you, and maybe now you can call an old friend. Apparently, we, young people, think we are the only ones who are smart.

I gave Mama Samuel something small and she quickly called one of the boys playing football on the road. Within five minutes, the boy bought two beers. Mama Samuel said she started drinking beer after she closed her bar. Before then, the only alcohol that passed her lips and touched her tongue was the Blood of Christ on Friday and Sunday every week.

I plan to see her again and ask her more questions. I will also try to get her number for you.

I love you so so much Tate Majina and thank you for convincing Baba to let me do my project here.

I miss you!

Your mwinjikulu,

Louise

~ Nine ~

WELL WATERS

A madman and a rich man are the same. The road is cleared for them like they own it. Their potential is feared. And behind their backs, many laugh at them, but few will have the courage to tell them the truth.

As a child, his mother told him to stay far from one of the streams of 'Sizi that many people called Machozi ya Mama. Its calmness had swallowed many children, and even when the soil got hard and covered in dust during the dry season, Machozi stayed full. Its water came from the tears of mothers whose children had been swallowed by Machozi. His mother did not want to join the woman who sat by Machozi until their eyes stopped swelling, their nose stopped running, and their hair started thinning.

When he was in secondary school, he was told something else by his philosophy teacher. He spoke of a man who once got rich from running a butchery across the country but used to live in a village on the mountain before that. In desperation, the man would leave his wife to walk all the way to Machozi and bathe in it with all his clothes before he lay bare and naked on the soil. He would roll three times to the left and then three times to the right. Once he had done that, he would lay still and whisper his desires to the falling moon and the rising sun. He had to stay still until the moon had finally slept. Once he opened his eyes, he was to look at the sun as he walked into Machozi to bathe and drink from. That is how he had gotten his money. The boy learned of this from their teacher six months before the teacher left the school to work for l'Etat in Kinshasa. The boy remembered how his teacher left wearing his fifteen-year-old crocodile that he only wore for special occasions: his marriage, school graduations, other weddings where he was invited specially, his children's baptism, communion, and confirmation. He wore a suit and a white shirt that had a high collar to hide the lumpy scar on the top right of his neck. His wife wore a headscarf with Mama Maria on it and the clothes she had worn three days before.

The boy would leave for Kinshasa four years later and become a man with a degree and a dream to shape his people for the better. He met many men and spoke with them about his dreams. At night, over Primus, they would agree and debate at length, but once the sun was awake and they met again indoors in suits and ties, the discussion was short, and none would give him work. He returned to his father's house and, in three months, began to work for his mother's cousin's brother-in-law.

The salary he received was enough to buy new suits, move from his father's home into the one-bedroom homes near the catholic university, and find a woman. Her father was an average commercant that had made just enough to send his ten children from different women to school. She was the first daughter and only living child of her father's first wife. He had many sons after her with other women, but she was the son he always went in search of.

Before her brother was born, her father taught her how to quickly count money and separate it into racks of dix mille francs. By age ten, she could buy, sell, and give change without using a calculator. She knew the feel of money well enough to know when Tonton Serge tried to give her fake money to follow him to Hotel Bonjour - a hotel with more customers during the day than at night. When Vital failed at managing her father's office, she did the work and let Vital receive praise the first time. The second time Vital came running to her for help, she let him sweat for a few days before helping him. This time, her father returned her brother, Vital, to a child from the young man he was becoming. It was a painful loss when he drank himself into 'Sizi, but his spirit had been broken long before that.

At school, she studied - well enough to pass as an average student and as the top student in her family. When her mother said it was time for her to marry, the girl, now a woman, refused. When her father agreed with her mother, she left for university. She washed clothes, cleaned houses and braided hair for all women, including Maman Honorable, to make money. It was with Maman Honorable that she learned how to choose a man and draw him near. It was with Maman Honorable that she learned of Kinshasa, Yaounde, Abidjan, and Dakar. Sometimes, Maman Honorable would give her a book to read: Fanon, Cesaire, Lopes, and Mariama Bâ.

Maman Honorable made her read because soon she would find a man, and he would make her stupid through love. The man would steal her brain and leave her with children to manage. There would be no more time for books. When they talked about the books, Maman Honorable reminded her not to be too smart. Men liked women stupid. When they, as the men, had an idea, women were never to challenge it. Instead, she was to applaud it, give him words of praise and marvel at his intellect- even if it was a ridiculous idea. Once adorned with praise, if the idea the man had proposed was fruitless, the woman was to discreetly plant a seed and allow for the man to discover the fruit of her labour. The reason why she needed to read was so she could be able to tell a bad idea from a good one. Maman Honorable believed a woman who was stupid or a woman who was too smart was more dangerous to herself than a woman who was smart enough to know when to be stupid.

And if the man did not have ideas or was a stupid man who only knew how to dress well, then the woman needed to be smart and teach her husband as she would her firstborn. And so, she kept reading, even after Maman Honorable was replaced. She sank herself into Delphine Zanga Tsogo's Vie de Femme and L'Oiseau en Cage, as well as Angele Rawiri's Fureurs et Cris des Femmes, whilst she waited to find a man- one who dressed well enough to be respected but not too shiny to be questioned.

School had finished, and many did not give a woman work as that was a man's job. She installed herself back in her father's shop selling suits and ties. Her father had let her stay only after he saw that more men stopped at his shop once they saw his daughter inside. Because there was no other man to fight, men would beat their chests by buying a suit in front of her for more than it should have been worth.

Her grandmother visited the shop once while she was selling to a customer. The man paid and left, but her grandmother asked how she could meet all these men and not manage to make a single one her husband. Her grandmother told her it was because she was smart but not as beautiful—ana pashwa angara. For two months, her grandmother applied a lotion that tickled and itched her whole body.

More men came into her father's store- then more women because they had heard of a girl who was stealing their husbands by selling suits to them. All men who walked into the store never left without buying a tie, at the very least, all except one.

He had come into the store and spoken with her. He needed a suit that was not black. They spent about half an hour looking at different suits. The man spoke about how the suit was important for his presentation to the government. Everyone wears a black suit, he needed a suit that was different, so he could be remembered. This was his opportunity to get to a position where he could change his town. He spoke of how he had read about Abidjan and the roads there had no potholes. Here in their town, there were more potholes than there were roads. She knew of Abidjan from Lopes' Tribalique. She knew it was as impressive as Kinshasa; they had good music and food, and their French was a bit different. They spoke about what their country was becoming, how young people were wasting away, and then he left. He did not find exactly what he wanted and said he would return in three days when there were new suits.

And like he had said, he came three days later just as the shop was about to close. He had been held back to do some unnecessary work by his uncle. They spoke about family. He told her he had a younger sister and his parents had remained married since his birth. He hid his surprise when she mentioned she was the first of ten children and laughed when she threatened she would pour hot water on a man that married her and had children elsewhere. He found the suit. He bought it. Then he married her. She stopped using her grandmother's lotion. She had found a husband, and she did not like the colour of her grandmother's hands.

He married her in the cathedral as her mother requested. It would bring honour to her name to have her daughter married in the cathedral after all the shame her husband had put her through. He wanted a simple wedding, but between his mothers and his wife-to-be, the wedding had more people than he knew. All of them claimed to know the couple and their families well.

They had enough goats to last them nine months. Somehow, the goats were eaten in three months with visits from in-laws and their in-laws. More goats came when she confirmed she was pregnant. Goat meat, cooked well, would feed anyone well except for a newborn child. When he knew she was carrying their child, he began to look for another job. His salary and the call money that came from her selling clothes and jewellery would not be able to take care of his child. For months he wore his sharpest suits, added a suit handkerchief that matched his tie, and kept his beard clean and short. When she stopped selling, spitting and continued to swell with carrying the child, he started talking to anyone who would listen.

It is at the most rare of times that a message from the past becomes a message for the present. For him, it was when watching her cry from her discomfort, Machozi ya Mama. He remembered his philosophy teachers as he held her. When she was soothed and asleep, he stepped out of his bed and left her asleep like he had done a few times before for work. His philosophy teacher followed him as he entered Machozi with his clothes then submerged his whole body in the water. His teeth clenched together as he wiped his face while walking back onto the banks of Machozi. He placed his clothes on the roots of one tree. The philosophy teacher said to roll three times to the left and then three to the right. He lay still. And he whispered his three requests over and over again.

To provide enough for his family.

To change his community.

To leave his children a legacy.

He heard the crickets and tsenene until they were stopped by the sun and bells of churches. He opened his eyes and walked into the river. When he finished, he put his damp clothes on and ran back to where he had left his wife. At the door he undressed and placed his clothes in a bucket of water, before entering his room. His wife moved slightly but did not seem to wake up.

The following week, he received a request to meet a man who was in charge of a government contract to build all the roads in the town. He met the man early in the evening after work. She had made fufu and sombe so he would not need food later. He met the man, and they spoke well. The man invited him to dinner at the end of the week. He and his pregnant wife matched the colours of their clothes like young couples do. The man and his wife welcomed and introduced them to his other friends. The pregnant woman greeted everyone like a young, respectful daughter of strangers, including Maman Honorable.

By the end of the month, he had left his uncle's business and become part of the strategy planning and monitoring team for the road project. When the child was born, they had moved away from the Catholic university to near the lake on La Belle Ave. She returned to selling clothes and jewellery to stay busy and active. When the money came, she reminded him of when they first met, of how they had spoken of Abidjan, Douala, and Dakar.

A month later, as they walked back from church, he spoke to her about how he had convinced the man to send him on business research trips to Dakar, Abidjan, and Douala to learn from them. When she went with him, she made friends who could buy her kitenge, boubou, kaftan, and superwax. She would use some of them to make wedding uniforms to sell in Beke. Every morning they were in Beke, he would still leave to visit Machozi.

The man finished the contract and went on to be deputy governor. The man asked him to follow, and he did. When the deputy governor became governor, he became deputy governor. By this time, their son was five years old. His wife had told him another child would not allow him to focus on the people and be a father. One was enough. When he asked for more children, she spoke to him about how their son's school did not have good books to learn from like they had used when they were back in school.

Then, the governor announced a plan to invest in new resources for all schools in their town. Worn buildings would be repainted, old benches and tables replaced, and scholarships were to be provided to the top performing students to study abroad in Senegal, Côte d'Ivoire, and Belgium. The scientists went to Belgium; social and humanities were too pro-African to imagine Belgium. The governor delegated the supervision of the project to his deputy governor. And so she became Mama Depute when they would visit the garçons and filles Beke in other countries.

Even with all the projects that they did, the député remained restless. He continued to visit Machozi every day. He did not notice that his clothes had been moved closer to the front door of their house. He had now built two houses, and ran a farm of cassava, beans, and pineapples just outside of Beke. His wife spent her time between raising their son, monitoring the farm, and the national visits required of her as Mama Depute. Occasionally, they would invite Maman Honorable and her husband to dinner along with the governor and his wife.

When the governor finished his term, the député received all the support from the rich Beke, Lebanese, Israeli, American, and French. His campaign was BekeFort- a people united and strong in improving their town. Beke was good. People's stomachs were full, their children were learning, and jobs were paying. The town was moving forward and so they voted for député to become Gouverneur. Mama Député became Mama Gouverneur with more national and international travels.

The new Governor started slowly by adding more to the projects he had worked on with the man. At the same time, he built tunnels underneath Palais du Gouverneur. It was for safe emergency exits, secret meetings, and so he could escape to Machozi without the bodyguards knowing. He taught his son about the different tunnels and the different things that he, as a father, had built for his son. He also tested him on books, even though he knew his mother had prepared him for the tests. As they lived in Palais du Gouverneur, he told his wife he went on morning walks to clear his mind for the day and see the town without the pretence it has when they see him as Gouverneur.

A madman and a rich man are the same. The road is cleared for them like they own it. Their potential is feared. And behind their backs, many laugh at them, but few will have the courage to tell them the truth. They both speak their truths freely and unbound by the same diplomacies that contain those in between. In the morning before the town woke up, he was able to see the town for what it was, even in the dark shadows. He could not tell her that he woke up in the morning to bathe in Machozi, roll in the soil, and whisper to the moon and sun so he could pay for her to travel to Abidjan.

In his second year, he began to change things even faster. BekeFort was about more than just ensuring children read in school and that people had jobs. Still, it was also about Les Enfants Beke investing in and owning their town. He nationalised businesses and organisations, took senior jobs from bazungu and gave them the right to Les Enfants Beke, who had learned kizungu zungu. With each replacement, he lost an investor. First, it was the Lebanese, then the Israeli. The Israelis pulled the Americans. The French funded his opposition and scared the rich Beke. Suddenly, people became hungry, teachers were not teaching children, and jobs were not paying. BekeFort became the talk of radios - not in support but in mockery. Mama Gouverneur supported her husband, but she no longer left the Palais du Gouverneur.

In desperation, the Governor ran to Machozi. He bathed in the water, stripped, rolled six times, and waited for the moon to fall. As he lay naked and bare, he heard a man singing ten steps from his head. The man got closer until he was right above. It started to rain, slowly, then faster than rain he had felt before. He was forced to open his eyes and saw the man who had been singing, naked, urinating over him.

An old man with small grey hair above his ears and bald at the top of his head. He continued to sing as he sat by the Governor's clothes. When the Governor went to grab his clothes, mwendabazimu slapped his hands. He tried again and his hands were slapped. Then, the man stopped singing and stared right into the naked Governor's eyes. He stood up from the clothes, never leaving the Governor's eyes, and walked right until their feet touched. The Governor knew that with baendabazimu, one never made fast movements when they were close. So, he stood still. The naked mwendabazimu hugged the naked Governor, then whispered in his right ear. And the Governor had no choice but to listen whilst being held by the man.

Mwendabazimu spoke of how proud he was of his student and what he had become. He warned the Governor to not visit Machozi again. Machozi would give him all these riches and dreams he wanted, but it would one day swallow - either his wife and child or him. If it was his wife and child, then he too would become mwendabazimu. Machozi would send his brother to swallow for Machozi. The Governor stopped listening to the madness. He had no brother, only a sister. Mwendabazimu bit his shoulder. The Governor pushed him away.

The Governor tried to return every day after that, but Mwend-abazimu was there before the moon fell and pissed on him. The Governor spent a month before returning to Machozi. And still, Mwendabazimu appeared. The moon had dropped, and the sun was still waking slowly. Mwendabazimu blocked him from bathing in Machozi again. In their dance by Machozi, he noticed that Mwendabazimu's beard did not grow as much on the right side of his face, with lumps on his neck below. He pushed Mwendabazimu far enough to run into the water and bathe. He needed Machozi to bring the Soviets and Chinese to save his town. The President had abandoned him. The other governors followed the President's decision. Other African countries would not touch him - their minds still carrying the freshness of Sankara's assassination and the state of Zimbabwe. They were not going to risk having the same fate.

The Soviets did not come. The Chinese did not come. The United Nations announced an emergency and created a mission. The Governor went to Machozi once, wept as he whispered, wept as he bathed, and then prayed after he dressed. Still, nothing happened. The following day, he sat by Machozi even after he had finished. There, he saw a line of military trucks rising just where pineapples used to grow four hills from the centre of town. He had no meeting scheduled with the military, but their speed told him to run. He arrived inside Palais du Gouverneur, his clothes soaked in more sweat than Machozi's water.

He told his wife to grab the suitcase as he woke up their son. It was the first suitcase he had bought for her when they had travelled. When they became député, they made the suitcase an emergency suitcase with enough clothes, money, a Nokia 1011, and property documents. When his son was dressed, he told him to show his mother the place where he used to go when they played cache-cache and to go to the very end.

By the time the General arrived, they were gone. He was asked of any last requests, and as a patriot, he would have spoken to his people to keep steady, but as a father, for the last time, he chose to call his wife.

"*Sarah, it's me. Did you take all you needed? Yes? Good. Give Sammi the phone. Samuel, you are doing good, mon ami. It's okay. Everything is going to be okay. Do you remember what I told you? You are now the man. Be the one I need you to be. Tell your mother I am sorry.*"

~ Ten ~

BLOOD NAME

But the purpose of a legacy is for it to continue. And for it to continue and not break down, it must be built upon.

I remember telling him, *"Come and have a beer with me, Papa. Just one. The children will be fine. We are both here. They are okay."*

He sat down at the table opposite me like he always had. This time he was a little less eager with his focus on the children playing on the balcony and in the garden behind me. No matter how old we get, the grey hairs, and the balding, there were some things that never left the both of us. He was trying to listen to me but the chewing of his inner left cheek gave him away, very much like his grandfather, Baba Luc.

"Papa, do you know why I never called you by your name all these years?" Silence. He was not expecting such a question from me.

On one occasion, I went to the barbershop with Papa and his mother's father. As they sat next to each other and the back of their heads faced me. Each cut made the folds of the grandfather's head more visible, and though younger and less pronounced, I saw the same folds in the back of Papa's head.

"We both know who you are named after, but you and I never spoke much about him."

When he was younger, Papa was chaotic, restless, and clumsy. If there was commotion, Papa was involved. If a glass broke, it was Papa. If someone's child was crying, it was Papa. For a long time, I held frustration and deep embarrassment about bringing Papa into any place. His carelessness over things and conversations created a deep-seated fear that one day, things would go horribly wrong. Ango, my friend, would pull me aside and remind me to be patient.

"My guy, you need to stop seeing him as just your father and realise he is a person- a human being."

My friend's words were true. Sitting there with Papa many years later, I saw it in the low hum under his words, the veins of the hands, and how he holds my hand when we walk. A firm, sure and confirmed hold.

"At first, it was because you frustrated me."

Three years after he passed away, Papa was born. As I remember, Papa pressed his lips together like his grandfather. Before I knew it, I was whispering his name to a new holder, Lionel. The name of a man who was long and wiry in frame with a quietness that invited others to pour their whole self into the room and him. When he entered rooms or bars after a day of wielding metals for street lamp poles, those there before him would nod in his direction. It was not the uncertain or dismissive nod quickly done to return to the conversation but the specific slow nod given to those well-known and often well-respected. After one beer, he would return home to his children and watch them work whilst waiting for his wife's own return from the market. Exuding a noble dignity and display of control that brought others to envy. Only the few who knew him before his voice met the ocean floor in its depth, knew of his troublesome childhood ways. Lionel was my father.

Unashamed of his emotions and expression, he would make it clear how he felt and what he would do. His impatience and clumsiness were not received as noble dignity like the one before him, but it was in that impatience that you saw the same fierce love. In some ways, I wonder whether those who knew who he was named after would have said the same about both of them. Papa was named after his father's father—my father. Lionel was my son.

For Lionel, growing up carrying the name of a man he had never met - yet everyone knew and expected him to become the same man- pushed him further from becoming this stranger as a child. Whenever his turbulence would start, his mother, Rachel, would sing a song to him. Before he turned 9, Rachel would sing.

"Katoto la-la!"

"Mimi katoto silali!" Papa would respond. They would repeat this song until Rachel saw Papa laughing or calm.

At 10, Rachel would start to sing Nakushukuru. And when Papa would see his mother start to pray, like the boy she had raised him to be, Papa would stop what he was doing, close his eyes and sing. By the time he was 14, he fought against God or the church.

He was no longer a small boy.

Rachel fought for a while. When she realised her boy was gone, she spoke to him the way elderly women spoke to young men. Instead of ordering or leading Papa, she would ask him questions that allowed him to be a man, yet underneath the questions, there was the reminder that no matter who he became, she was his mother.

"Uko mutoto wa?"
"Muhigirwa." Papa would respond.

"Usha kwa mushamuka si vile?"
"Yes Mummy."

"Kuji?" Rachel would say it under her breath.
"Shusha." Papa finished.

When it was too much for Rachel, she would spend nights in her Bible, before she spoke to me.

"Luc, you need to talk to your son."

How many times had my mother told my father this when I, too, was Papa's age? The evenings when he would come back from work, hand over his brown leather bag and sit in his red armchair with golden knobs. He would undo his shoelaces, one shoe after the other and place them by the right front leg of the chair. He would put the socks he had taken off and ball up into the left shoe. Then he would call me to bring him a glass and bottle of the wine he had left in the fridge, just like I did with Papa. White wine was the way we said there was a discussion that needed to be had. I just never lectured Papa as long as my father had lectured me.

Mama LouLou used to tell me that Papa's namesake had gotten his behaviours, mannerisms and lectures from Baba Edison. We never called Ba Mukubwa Tate because he never let us. It really started with my father.

When he was younger, Ba Mukubwa had agreed to be responsible for my father when Tate had told him of her plans to return home, not to Beke, but to BaNidunga. Ba Tate was no longer needed as much since Ba Mukubwa had taken over the petrol stations. Mama LouLou used to tell me how Ba Mukubwa and Tate used to spend hours in his office as Tate explained every single document to him. So when he left with Tate, Ba Mukubwa became Baba for everyone including my father, yet he always reminded them that he was their brother and not their father. Even with this distinction, LouLou still knew to call him Baba and not Kaka or Grand as my father did.

For Ba Mukubwa, he wanted his youngers to know that they still had a duty to Ba Tate. During school times, he made sure that they called Ba Tate at least twice a week. First was a family call to discuss how the stations were doing and to pray together. I had been to some of these calls that always took about two hours between the Swahili news at 7 p.m. and the English news at 9 p.m. The second call was between each person and ba Tate.

When they were not in secondary school boarding for the long holidays, he would divide their holidays in two. During the first half, my father would follow Ba Mukubwa to the petrol stations. Still, instead of sitting in the office drinking tropical fruity, my father was made to work with all the others, washing and cleaning cars, filling petrol into cars, and watching over the fuel tanks during the refilling. My father did the same with me. He explained that it was the way Ba Mukubwa had taught him to learn everything about the business, including how much it cost the staff to buy lunch from Mama Tracy around the corner.

In the second half, he sent all of them to BaNidunga to help ba Tate with their farms. They would be sent alone without any parents, and my father was responsible for Ya Louise and Ya Edison. The first time he was responsible for them during a trip was when he first started secondary school, but before ba Tate returned to BaNidunga. My father took Ya Louise to Beke because Ba Mukubwa had refused for her to go with Ba Tate. And though Ya Louise and Ya Edison saw my father as an older brother, these trips made him more of their Tonton. He showed them how to work on the farms, the secret to making good mashanza, and how to catch and prepare rabbits.

Because he had watched over them when they had gone to the farms, Mama Edison -or as my father knew her, Da Bebe – left my father to watch over Ya Edison and Ya Janvier the day her own mother died. Ba Mukubwa and his brother Baba Edison escorted Da Bebe to bury her mother. Her only other blood relative, other than her own two children Edison and Janvier. The discipline of working on the farms and in the petrol station structured him always to learn fast. He spent the rest of his time at the station when he wasn't raising Ya Louise, Ya Edison, and Ya Janvier. At the same time, Ba Mukubwa spent less and less time at the station, knowing that all he needed to do was call my father.

It was through my father's ideas and his learning of the changes in technology that Ba Mukubwa could expand the number of petrol stations, buy property, and invest in other businesses in Kampala, Nairobi, Abidjan, and Accra. These did not happen all at once but very slowly. When they invested in Kampala, my father heard about the business in Nairobi, which he followed. When he got to Nairobi and found companies that

Ba Mukubwa would like, they told him about Accra. And in Accra, he came across an Ivorian who sweet-talked him into the fashion industry.

When he was confident that all businesses were stable under my father, Ba Mukubwa decided to enjoy old age with Mama LouLou at their farm. The first thing my father did was begin to build the Maisha Foundation, which we know today.

Papa, like his namesake, was raised for a good part of his life in the absence of his father's physical presence. I was always travelling between different fields and farms, trying to build a name for myself. Build my legacy outside of my father. Rachel raised this boy, and whenever I would get back, I would be frustrated because, to me, I saw no change. I didn't know that when I was away, Papa would sit at the table until his sister Anna's homework was finished. I didn't know he had fixed walls and ensured that Rachel's small farm stayed in shape. When young hooligans came to menace them about unpaid bills in the neighbourhood, I found out that it was Papa who they had listened to and left people alone.

I was so focused on trying to make Papa just like my father that I ignored all the rest. But the purpose of a legacy is for it to continue. And for it to continue and not break down, it must be built upon. Lionel, Baba, my father made his legacy and built this school for all of you here today. Papa, Lionel, my son, comes back to this very ground having studied, worked, and built his own business that will see that every single one of you and every single child that comes through this school will have the guarantee of having school fees paid here and at the best universities in Africa.

They are telling me that I must step away from the microphone now, but I am an old man and still have a lot to say and not as much time to say it all. Many people will speak and remember my Papa's success and who he is today, but I share this story with you for three reasons.

First, to remind you all that it is always a journey and that even if you seem to have it all together, your own challenges will come. So be steady, brave, patient, and commit to winning those challenges.

Second, every experience, memory, and encounter is a lesson. You may not understand it today, but take deep value in what you come across in your lives. You never know when you just might need that lesson later on.

The third and last key point is that we are inheritors of names. And with those names comes a history and, more importantly, a legacy. Whether good or bad, we must not be trapped and stuck in one place by the weight of that inheritance, but we must look beyond it. Where the inheritance is bad, we must use it as a reminder of what and where not to go ever again so that it keeps us on the path for the better. Not smooth paths. Trust me, Papa had some very bumpy roads like the ones in Mbarara, but they were full of good fruits that bring us here today.

Where the inheritance is good, like you have inherited these opportunities, you must look to build on top of that foundation in your own way. Take Papa's legacy as a challenge—a challenge for you to grow from it and add yours to it so that there are many good legacies to be inherited. Don't wait to build it tomorrow; start right this second.

Before they chase me, I want to call Papa to join me.

Son, one day, I pray that a day arrives when you also will get to feel what I am feeling today with your children. Aksanti mutoto wangu.

TIMELINE

Patterns in the Dust: Tracing the Footsteps of History

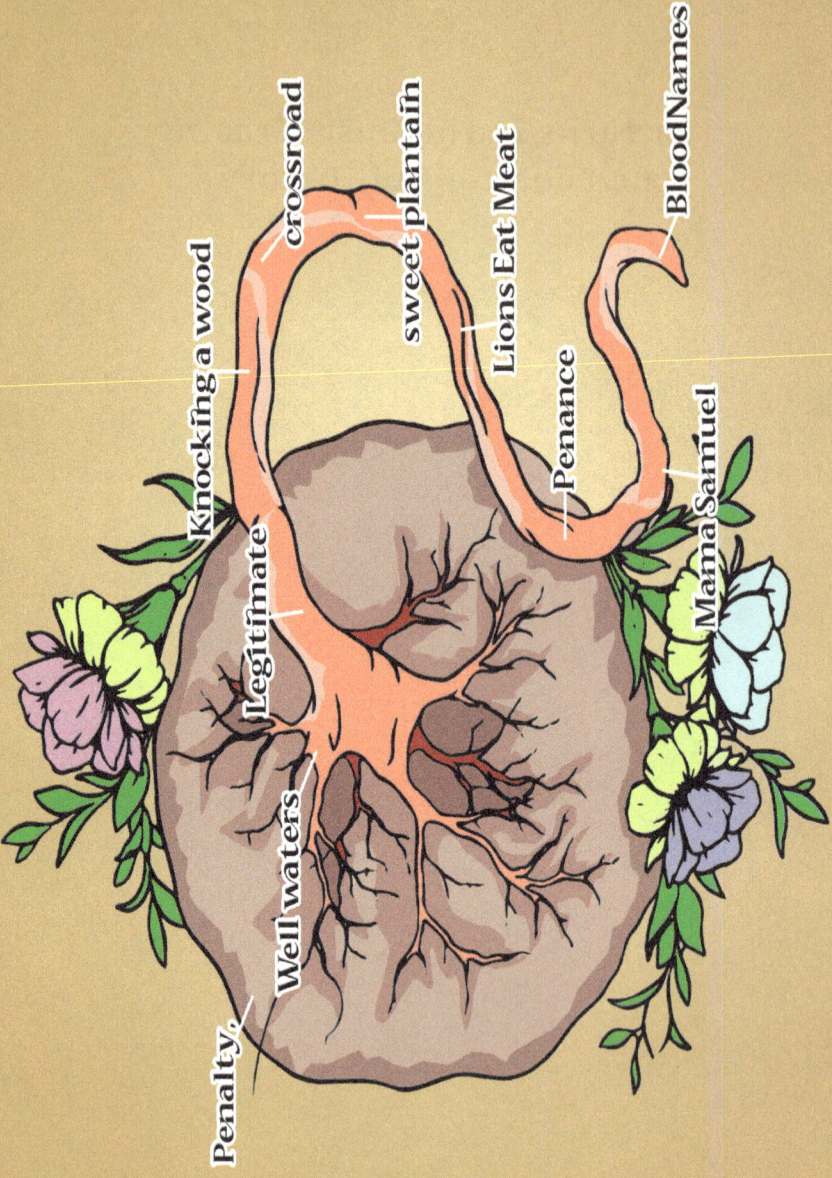

~ Eleven ~

KANYONYA - AN INTRODUCTION TO SIRI YABO

A mountain is born. A girl speaks to snakes. A man eats flesh. Every town has its secrets that are never really secrets. Secrets that are true. Secrets that are myths. And secrets that were never true. *Siri Yabo* returns to Beke Town as the second collection in the *United Front* trilogy to uncover the secrets of the past and the future.

He was found with his mouth on the thighs of a woman. Every five seconds, he would lift his head away from her thighs and spit. From that day, many girls and women were told to never visit him alone, and if they must see him, they had to cover all of their bodies and eat food that would make the mouth smell. Papa Dokolo was only called Papa Dokolo to his face, but everyone knew him as Kanyonya.

He had lived at the top of the hill ever since he left his father's home to make one of his own with his wife Maria. She had married the carpenter's son who many did not speak to, but she saw a focus in him that many men who rushed to speak to her did not have. As the sun woke the hill, Maria would walk down step by step until she reached the market to sell jewellery. Young girls who had begun to learn the eyes of men and bodies, too, would find Da Maria for a necklace, a bracelet, and a set of waist beads. When the market would begin to sleep, she would make her way to the lake to collect beads and shells from Aganze. They would talk about the fish in the lake, how far he had to go to find fresh big fish, and if he had caught enough to feed his ten children. Then, after sharing his portion of the money she had made, Maria would walk back up the hill with her beads and shells to spend the evening making more as she watched over Papa Dokolo's food on the fire. Papa Dokolo never came down the hill but would go over it into the forest where they had said women gave birth to children and left them for tree roots, snakes, and dogs. He would leave before Maria and return after the sun had sunk and few still had their fires burning. In the darkness, he would still find his way to the fire Maria was burning, and place the wood he had cut close to the fire but out of the view of their wooden gate. Wiru always came to houses unannounced, and if he saw the wood, the whole village would climb to the top of the hill to ask Papa Dokolo for the wood he had cut to keep his wife warm.

Yet, they were the ones who laughed when the rains came, and the mud slid from the tip of the hill and pushed against the mud of his walls until the water seeped through and kissed his and Maria's feet. It was then that he would use the wood he had cut to block the holes where the water had eaten into the mud. What was left of the wood was then used to raise their bed higher. The water had sat and eaten into the wood by the time the rains finished. It could not be used for the coming rains. Burning it would bring more smoke than fire, so Papa Dokolo would carry the water-eaten wood back up the hill and into the centre of the forest, where many did not go except for Mpanga boy, who collected the best wood to keep his bedridden mother warm. Here, he would place the wood next to the ones he had placed after the rains the year before. The soil would finish what the water had started.

As he turned around to leave, the Mpanga boy raised his hand to show Papa Dokolo what else his mpanga had cut. Papa Dokolo turned back, placed his wood on the ground, collected four pieces of wood, and sat down by the Mpanga boy to start a fire. Mpanga boy asked Papa Dokolo about his side of the hill, and Papa Dokolo told him what he knew from Maria since he himself rarely spent time in town.

They had said the meat he sold were bodies of people he had drank blood from. He had sacrificed his wife Maria through witchcraft to gain his powers and become rich. Some had heard that it was virgins and barren women that he drank from to make him rich and live longer. When women and girls went missing, people would whisper *Kanyonya. Still, no* one ever confronted him for fear that they or their children would also go missing....

THE DOTS

Uki kumbuka kwenye
unatokea uta jua kwenye una
enda.

In 2014, I was sitting in an auditorium in a school in Johannesburg, listening to peers present on where they would see themselves in the future. Each person shared intimate, vulnerable and fascinating dreams, but the one person I will never forget is Chebet Naserian. Today, the concept may not be as mind-blowing to some, but back then, she spoke of different things she would want to do, such as making a chocolate factory, being an artist, and empowering and collaborating with other women. All disjointed and separate points until her conclusion showed us where she would end up. And how, by connecting the dots backwards, all the things she had done or is currently doing would lead to it. So, if you have not already made the connection, this section, The Dots, takes inspiration from Chebet's 2014 presentation.

It is also fitting to have this at the end because I have never been a fan of starting things with Your Excellency, Honourable, Ingenieur, Odugwu, Madam, All Protocols Observed. However, I most definitely believe in the importance of gratitude, acknowledgement, and citation.

I have been fortunate to be around many storytellers with different approaches. In my father, I learned the quality of telling a story in a form that carried a philosophical feel and seriousness, yet simultaneously being able to completely change the script with some of the wittiest and funniest remarks. In my mother, I learned how to embed a story within a story and pass a message to the intended person without being overt. I also learned that a hyperlink to anything related or unrelated is always possible - it is all about delivery. I have grown with many people over time, but there are three that remain dear and near to me. In my brother, the one that comes before, I learned to bring a story to life in another's mind through the countless nights we shared a room, and he spoke of his sport's victories. In my sister, the one who comes after me, I learned how to enjoy a story as you tell it and take one on a journey without having to beat around the bush. In my sister, the one that comes after her, I learned that in every story, there is always more than one road in telling and in listening, and that is where another story can be birthed. Among the Sanginga, the Mwarirho, and many others, I have also learned of infinite stories which have brought me here.

Outside of them, there are several people for whom this journey would not have been possible. Sister Patricia and JayyDubb, through their practice and time, have imparted much wisdom in creating such worlds. Atlese should be a co-author for this, having read every version there possibly could have been and gently pushing for what could be. I can never quite explain how her mind has unravelled this journey for me. Annette, because there are enemies of progress and agents of change - and she is the latter. A world like FBW only came true from a world she created and a shelf that always remained new. Binta is an artist in denial and, through conversations with her and her eye for detail with purpose, has brought many needed pensive nights on where my work should speak.

Jelani and John. There are some people who can spend hours on what may seem like wild nonsense to the outside ear. These two have been the reasons for many words heard by the 4 a.m. wind. Clémence for astute, stubborn and persistent diplomacy convinced me to return to art and creation at a time when I had very much rolled down my sleeves and closed the top button. Efua because sometimes the answers I needed were in the questions we planted. Ihunanyachukwu, the whole story about her, is one that I have promised to tell on the mountain-tops and the bottoms of oceans. Still, this door is open because of the simple gesture of sitting and listening that she did. Nana, because through her, I have been reminded that laughter, love, and accountability are only possible with all else that is present, and that, too, must be acknowledged. There, too, we must stand for ourselves and each other. Dubie, for living, being and writing fiercely and proudly about who was, who is and who will be in our communities even when no one is looking. Ibby, because there is never a right time and place for a story to be told, whether it be in the grid of Apple City or beside the night buses for the NHS workers. Ijay is a passion that does not have to be loud so long as we are focused and committed. Jason Jackson, because when there is the temptation to retreat into ease and comfort, it is his boldness that I draw on. Salima lives next to or with quality and hope, and those hand in hand can dent a droplet of water. Leanna rides waves with a firmness akin to the ground that carries that water. Her unwavering faith that we will land and arrive in pursuit of us and all that we are. I would include these names in the following sections, but their stories (of which there are many) are still being written.

There is a saying that I once saw, funnily enough, on a Tusker Baridi billboard on the turn of Convent Drive and James Gichuru Road. Uki kumbuka kwenye unatokea uta jua kwenye una enda. If you remember where you came from, you will know where you are going. If you have read this far, you have read where we have gone with stories, but the following pages are remembering some of the places and the people of where we, well, I, in this instance, have come from. The following pages give some sort of answer to a question my father ingrained in me - why?

TATE TINA

"Uta onea ku batoto yako"

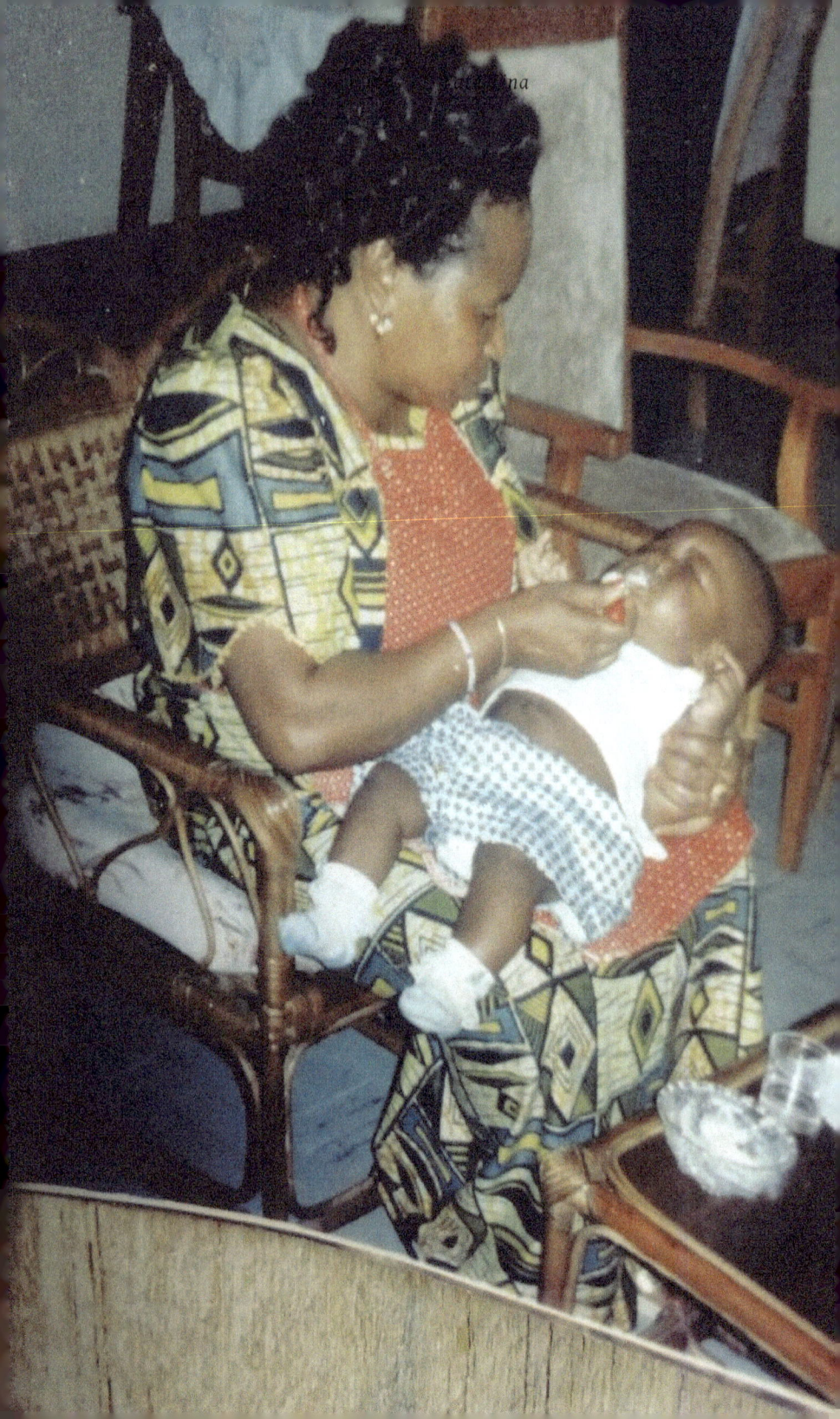

This work and this body are, in many ways, because of Tate Tina. Tate muzala Mama. I have heard stories from so many people, but none that sit with me the way that Tate Tina's stories do. Perhaps it has to do with an unexplainable connection.

As I completed this work, I got the fortune of spending about a month with her and realised how much the stories she told were simply life. Her telling them was orienting others whilst passing on parts of her story. And for me and those who come from her, it also passed on parts of our own story to us. She is an archivist with an acute sense of when to release things she has stored in her archives. It extends beyond stories, as my time with her showed me she has many photos of moments that have never been seen before. These photos that I now have are a story for another day.

When Tate Tina tells her stories, she tells them with a matter-of-fact honesty. It is not brutal honesty because that term is quite rough and contains a shock factor. In my opinion, some of her stories have been told at the most random of times. Though some were surprising, they were not feather-ruffling in how brutal honesty is delivered. It was simply honest. Whether it was about how she and her Innocent built their home, what she managed to buy at the market, or how she witnessed women, men, young boys, and girls walk through this journey called life. She was not crass with it, but she was also not filtered. And as she laid the story for one's heart and mind, it was for them to decide what to do with it. Her part had been done.

This work is dedicated to her because it tries to do in writing what she does daily - talk about life and live it. From Birthing Waters is fictional, yet it draws its flow from the rhythm in Tate Tina's stories. In writing From Birthing Waters, contend with who, rather what, comes from the waters of birth. This was to directly speak to a saying that Tate Tina says quite frequently - at least to me.

"Uta oneya ku batoto yako."

At face value, her statement may feel like the purpose of children is to ensure a better life for oneself. Children are their guarantee of a second life. And for those who need it and can sustain it healthily - it can be. For Tate Tina, it is really about personal conviction and resolution. The internal questions arise on whether one has done enough, done their best, done what is right and should have been done, and whether the sacrifices were worth it. Whether... the list is endless.

She has done what she believed was good for others in her life and through what she witnessed. Sometimes, the act of goodness or kindness was met with hardness or a response not similar to goodness. She asked herself whether what she did was good or bad in those moments. And at that moment, it would sit with her. Many years later, she would see how someone or the other would help her child because of an act she had done decades ago and forgotten.

She has experienced great losses in consecutive seasons. She carries the loss in different ways, and it encroaches on her life for brief moments. Yet, she still speaks of how her children - all of them not just biological - have gifted her with so much resolve and joy in who they are, have become, and are becoming.

It is from these waters where she birthed—in the midst of love, pain, sacrifice, and goodness—that she has gained momentum to carry on beyond herself. Something unexplainable happens in those birthing waters, and even more, comes from it than just a child.

Tate Tina when she was being courted by Tate Konda. This
is the photo he sent to his in-laws.

TATE M'NKINGI

As a child, my mother was a picky eater. I know this for certain, not because I was physically there to witness her as a child, but because of Tate M'Kingi. The mother to the mother of my mother. I know she did not lie because I confirmed it three times with my mother (the beauty of growing up with a father and a set of uncles who are all scientists; three becomes a special number).

My first memory of Tate M'Nkingi is of a skinny woman who remains tall for her age. Her strictness manages to keep her spine upright and not hunched over. I got the sense she was more expressive when she was younger, but with her old age and her children now fully grown adults with adult children of their own, others could shout. Her daughter, Tate Tina, got her stance, sharp eye stare, strictness, and vast knowledge from Tate M'Kingi.

I am a sucker for stories and good ones at that. Nollywood, gossip, series, and stories of people before I knew them. A story will keep me glued still for hours, which used to scare adults around me. I was the type of child no one ever wanted to go silent. If I was silent, it was because I was trying to figure out if blankets are flammable - blame action movies. Or, I got bored and left for a family friend's house - much to the horror and despair of my father's younger brother on one occasion.

Well, when we used to go to Tate Konda and Tate Tina's place, I would greet everyone and sit still for all the exchanges about how big we, the children, had become. Once I felt the eyes from the adults had relaxed, I would slide away to see Tate M'Nkingi.

The setup of Tate Konda and Tate Tina's home made running around and playing in fun. At the time when I used to run to see Tate M'Nkingi, the very front of the compound was a small bungalow that served as a bar in my mother's younger days. The bungalow bar also holds a fascinating story connection - one of the very few I have - to Tate Sanginga Muzala Papa. The house is built inside a small hill; at the top is where all the main quarters are. Then, at the back, at the bottom of the hill, there is a bathroom and two bedrooms, and the real kitchen is where the cooking takes place. There was enough space to play around the house on any side, and depending on where one was standing, it was possible not to hear a child playing on the other end. This sometimes meant people looked for me around the house for a good 20 minutes before I was eventually found sitting on a stool by Tate M'Kingi's bed. A place I had been for hours.

Unknown to me at the time, Tate M'Nkingi had gotten sick, and her presence at Tate Konda and Tate Tina's home was so they could watch over her and her health. I think she just liked to sleep and rest a lot because she was old, even when someone would walk in with a glass of water and some medicine. To this day, I don't know what she was facing, and there is a comforting peace in that - of course, until a doctor gives me a form to fill regarding my family's health history.

Tate M'Kingi centre wearing the headscarf.

It was probably one or two hours of listening to her tell stories, but every time I was called away from her because we were leaving, it felt like she was only starting to tell her story with me hunched over in my stool. She would talk about how she used to make sure she always had fruits in her home, especially during school holidays, because finding food that Dada could eat was difficult, but she accepted fruits and bishimbo.

She would not just tell me the story from point A to point B to point C. Sometimes, she asked questions to me. Did I know how they grew particular fruits? Was Dada still as picky with her food? Was I picky with my food? She would also invite me to ask her questions. In my fascination with wanting to know about where I came from, my questions always leaned towards family. In her case, she was not able to tell me more about her biological parents, who passed on when she was still young, but she told me about everyone else. How each of her children were whilst they were growing up. My Tate was her first. She was strong and disciplined because she even managed to deal with Tate M'Nkingi's strictness - which she undoubtedly inherited, along with her ability to keep all her white clothes white from sunrise to sunset. She spoke of her brother briefly, but her children and grandchildren were the stories she shared that created another world for me.

In her passing, one of the things I now miss is the chance to have the elders around me humanised. Often, there is this Morgan Freeman effect - not that they have always been old, but that this is just how they have always been. It is hard to think of them having done other things with their lives except for what they do now. Tate's stories allowed me to glimpse them and their lives before me. Some stories explained some things about them, and others did not - or at least left me with more questions.

The quality I drew from her, which I still need a lot of practice in refining, is the ability to tell the simplest of events or information in the most captivating ways. In hindsight, her stories, in terms of content, did not have a "wow factor." She climbed a tree and got avocados for her granddaughter. Simple. Straight-forward. Smooth. But the way she told the story - I would feel like I was witnessing a Genevieve Nnaji, Ramsey Nouah, and Omotola Jalade-Ekeinde love triangle. In her, I learned there was no need to go fishing for bombastic words to make a story.

PAPA GANG

There is nothing funny about
funny stories - sometimes.

With a lot of my elders, the ways stories were told were never direct. The story's message was clear and direct, but the way it was told or delivered to the intended audience appeared not to be on the surface level. I hold so many memories of our parents sitting with us in a circle and telling us stories. To those whom the message in the story was not meant for, the story would simply just register as a story being told spontaneously. The intended, however, would receive the message. And this was true of Papa Gang's stories.

Since memory calls, or at least since I learned how to sit or stand still and listen to people speak, his stories have been the funniest. Early on, I would always bid farewell to him with my cheeks tired, my chest full, and my mind buzzing with more questions to get more stories from him.

Though I now have the fortune of adding some centimetres to my height, Papa Gang was and remains a giant of a man who I understood - quite early on - that he is not a man to be messed with. If someone crossed him, he finished the matter. I never crossed him myself because I witnessed others who had. There was also really no chance for me to cross him because, as a lover of stories, he is a library to me. Through him, I know a great deal more about my fathers as boys and young men. At the same time, I have learned about the quantity of food, how meat was shared, and the range and measures of discipline parents of my fathers and mother took. In these stories, some were light-hearted, grim, and serious. What became clear with his stories was that humour and laughter do not have to be negated and can exist alongside the seriousness of a story. Stories that are serious do not always require a serious tone to be told, shared, and understood. Papa Gang can tell stories about 1995 to 1998, have a listener in tears from laughing, and still understand the gravity of the events being told. Without intending to, he showed me how humour and comical relief can be weaved into stories without disrespecting the events or taking away from it. The message still passed clearly.

In his stories, I drew some of the humour I tried to infuse into scenes that could have simply been written in a straight-serious way.

There are stories that I will never be able to read in books or find online trying to research them, but through him, many of those searches have been answered. That gift came with a reminder to have at least one person, if not many, open to sharing memories and stories of who they were, who they are, and who they see themselves becoming as a community. Papa Gang was that person for me with my fathers. It was not a title or a role that he was given or told to do. It just naturally happened that he became someone who told me stories about how my community, especially my fathers, became who they are as I know them. There are keepers of stories and memories, which are just as important as tellers of our stories. Papa Gang is one. There are many others, whether knowingly or unknowingly, who change the course of those who come after by sharing what came before. Mama Honorable is one. It may read like such a minor role, but the weight of what she shares is undeniable - much like Papa Gang.

MRS KIMUTAI

"We are not doing things just because it says so in the book. We must do it because it makes sense, and you mean it."

I tell the story of Mrs Kimutai at least 12 times a year because, in many ways, it is an unforgettable turning point. Fresh, young, and quite big headed going into high school I managed to find myself in an English class with Mrs Kimutai. She was my first English teacher that was not white since Kindergarten at Ainembabazi in Kabale, Uganda a decade before. And in hindsight, I believe she knew this about many of the students who passed through her class and took that responsibility seriously. As one of our first assignments in her class, Mrs Kimutai asked us to write a short story within Cambridge's 250 to 350-word style. The prompt had something to do with an apple. Roughly 95% of us wrote about a story based on communities we had never been in. I wrote about snow, brunettes, blonds, and blue eyes. In response, Mrs. Kimutai gave many of us 2 out of 25 grades. The highest may have been a 7 out of 25, but the red pen she used only left panic in my mind. Dad was going to be mad, and I had no clue how to explain what I did wrong to get this grade or how I intended to improve to make sure it never happened again. That was until Mrs Kimutai explained that there is nothing wrong with telling stories about snow and blue-eyed people, but because we lack that experience, the stories we write are predictable and, in some aspects, overdone. Yet, we all have backgrounds and experiences that could write so many stories.

Mrs Kimutai threw out the curriculum timeline and took us through a six-week process of writing short stories, editorials, and several articles about the places we come from. She also required us to deliver presentations on research that we had done about the places we came from. It is here that I wrote my first full story, Betrayed, and where equally my interest in post-conflict reconciliation took root. We know our stories, but until then, they had never really been placed at the forefront of my learning and given the time to breathe into their fullness. Although there was Chinua Achebe's No Longer at Ease and Ngũgĩ wa Thiong'o's The River Between, it was not until Mrs Kimutai demanded it and created such a space that I took a stab at penning a story grounded in cultures and communities that I come from and live in.

We still read Shakespeare and quite frankly enjoyed it because Mrs Kimutai could mould a story to our context instead of oneself to the story. What do chapati, Brutus, quencher, and 20 bob have in common? Ask Mrs Kimutai. Before her, it was the subversive requirement to leave oneself at the door of the classroom, all the history, the baggage and the knowledge that came with being who I was. In her class, she pushed us to bring everything to the table: how we read, wrote, and communicated. The fear of shame in reading a context that Cambridge had stated firmly as betrayal took on multiple layers. How many Brutus versions have I lived through? How does it change the context of understanding the dynamic present? Her push to give herself wholly to the creative without separation went beyond the English classroom and into the theatre.

Mrs Kimutai directed my last play at this institution. It was a play written by the late Great Jamaican-British Benjamin Zephaniah titled Listen to Your Parents that takes one through the experience of Mark - a young boy who dreams of becoming a poet and playing for Aston Villa. However, in this, his experience at home with his parents and particularly the father figure - who Jazz Moll played (there is a story of this man for another day). I played Mark. A sensitive and vulnerable character, but my approach to embodying that was a terribly copy-paste of a dramatic Hollywood film with little weight behind it. During one scene when Mrs Kimutai doesn't believe it, she stops and says, "*We are not doing things just because it says so in the book. We must do it because it makes sense, and you mean it.*" She asked us to draw from experiences we know of and, if we lacked any, to imagine that we were living the situation our characters were in with our loved ones. Then to dig deep and find how we would respond in such a situation. What situation, you ask? Read the play. Mrs Kimutai is why I have been banned from looking at my mother during any creative performance she attends. One of the monologues Mrs Kimutai and I had worked on heavily brought her to tears.

There were also terms that she brought up that also echo through every time I write. One of them was "verbal diarrhoea". Verbal diarrhoea was Mrs Kimutai's way of reminding us that we did not need to always use long sentences and big words that give one a headache trying to remember their meaning. Instead of "*He was cantankerous and cataclysmically venomous*" one could say, "*He was bad mannered and destructive.*" Straightforward, clear, and keeps the momentum going. Of course, the goal was not to be simple but to be able to ensure that complex choices were made because they were necessary and made sense. It is not because I read a new word in the book I just finished that I must now sprinkle it in every other sentence and paragraph. Verbal diarrhoea!

Through her, I learned that mastery and understanding were not just about understanding the complex aspects and big words but also the simple aspects and the common words. Equally, Mrs Kimutai was and remains a living model of how culture weaved into the language provides another layer. From Birthing Waters was sparked by many things, but it was sharpened into what it is now by the constant reminder of Mrs Kimutai to be intentional with my work and not to just "verbally diarrhoea" everywhere because I know English.

TSHIMUNDU

His presence in the making of
From Birthing Waters and beyond
has explained to me the depth
of brotherhood.

For as long as I have known him or of him, he has always been of his own mind. I hold a memory of him from about 20 years before writing this. I had just finished playing an away game football match and happened to remember that Tshimundu went to this school from a conversation our mothers had had. So I went in search of him and found him coming from doing some P.E. It was a brief hello, and we went our separate ways. We weren't the closest of kids, though we knew of each other's families. His brother, who had the biggest smile and laugh, and the giant who did not play around - put us in our place with one look. What was fascinating about him at that point was his choice of hairstyle. A hairstyle that on any other child would have been cause for severe bullying, but he radiated such an impenetrable confidence and charisma with it that everyone just went with it. And all I could think about as a child was

"How does he do it?"

And so, on the pitch, as we walked our separate ways, I really wanted to find out what this kid thinks. It only took about 16 years to begin to find out.

At some point during a long reflection, one of the many things that transitioning into a new chapter requires, Tshimundu, came to mind. And by the ease of the internet, we were able to reconnect. We then worked together for a year as part of a start-up. And I followed his work quite closely - both in and outside of the startup.

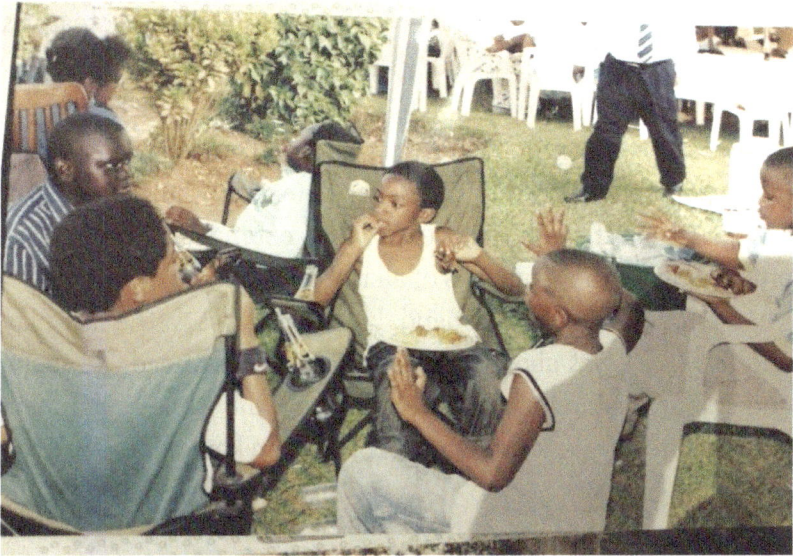

L-R: Aurelie, Alain, Beryl, Kevine, Tshimundu (Centre),
Nteranya, Daniel 'Kat'

There was good banter, the occasional share of exciting opportunities and other cool creatives. By this time, I had not been
able to dance at the frequency that I had used to. In part because
I had somehow convinced myself that abandoning creativity
would provide me with more concentration to push through an
academic program I could not stand. At the same time, I was
filled with a certain rage and distaste for the program and a
recent dance experience, respectively.

However, in the lockdown and forced conditions for reflection, people like Annette, Jelani, John and Binta unknowingly set
a train through the recurring conversations of investing back
into the arts. I dabbled here and there, but I also heard someone
telling me that I had to choose and that creativity was not the
right choice. A foolish dream. And since I listened to the voice
for myself, where I could not dive into being creative myself, I

would invest deeply into other creatives. Among the creatives in my village was Tshimundu.

And in true Tonton fashion, Tshimundu's role was quite the uno reverse card or J-retour in Inter-demande. I had laid out my plan, such as the way one sets out an extended play in Inter, after studying the strategies of all the other players. In this case, I had studied the plays at hand, but when I got to the last play and felt like I was about to win, Tshimundu changed the shape and colour, making it impossible to leave the game as planned. He added to my deck in the next round, and kept adding to keep me in the game.

Mid-2022, a particular conversation I had been a part of circa 2017 - 2018 came to mind. Marlon James explained a part of his writing process and how he built forms of discipline in it by allocating specific times to writing. These were times that he would strictly abide by for writing. I could do something similar for creatives by being a soundboard and an accountability person for Tshimundu. I proposed having regular creative sessions where - unknown to him at the time - Tshimundu would work on his creative projects, and I could contribute where possible. All so that the village could get more Tshimundu work.

Something I know now that he does and did back then is to laugh in gentle agreement. His agreement is long term, but the terms of that agreement were very temporary. He would begin to facilitate sessions where he put me to work—two times a week for one hour and thirty minutes over the course of more than six months. The only things accepted in those sessions were vulnerable banter and creativity. He respected that with a deep seriousness.

This is what happens when Tshimundu flips the script.

His consistency and unwavering dedication to showing up and being charged to go as deep as work demanded prevented any surface-level attempt at creativity. I am as stubborn as a Congolese Tonton, and most times, I can slip away from something with the upper hand. But Tshimundu is another Congolese Tonton, and he has challenged me in my work for months. In the moment, I hadn't noticed how his Tonton methodology managed to build more and more self-confidence about the creative work.

His thoughtfulness in engaging with creative work, his reflections, and his questions brought about conversations that define and ground this chapter of my creative work. I need to have more focused intentionality in what my creative work should be, yet not limit it from what it can possibly be. Louise's letter originated from a challenge by Tshimundu to write in the first person. When I would go on about a certain work and want to discontinue it, Tshimundu would respond with a Tonton's, *"Mais pourquoi?"* Or something in that realm.

If not for anything else, *From Birthing Waters* needs to recognise Tshimundu as the maker of the time from where it came from. All of the chapters in FBW started, expanded, and/or found their end in the presence of Tshimundu and the time he spared.

As a history lover, Tshimundu's presence in the making of *From Birthing Waters* and beyond has explained to me the depth of brotherhood.

He is the unsuspecting brother-in-arms.

Merci Yaya.

YANN & VERT PUBLISHING

We were not always like this,
and it is important to recognise
our journey for the part it has
played in dreams, brotherhood,
manhood, and selfhood.

The power of *"Yes, it can be done,"* is so incredible. And even more so when it is from someone least expected. Yann and Vert Publishing is a story I think of as the spirit of going together on a journey of separate dreams.

Yann holds a lot of love, and a conversation of ours in more recent times has never concluded without waves of emotions, honesty out of respect, and serious bouts of laughter. It may sound like this dynamic would clearly explain how we arrived at a discussion where he entrusted me with writing the first book to be released by Vert Publishing and how I would entrust him with my first-ever complete set of works.

We were not always like this, and it is important to recognise our journey for the part it has played in dreams, brotherhood, manhood, and selfhood.

Before 2012, I feared Yann for multiple reasons that I am unable to disclose now. At the same time, there was also a deep admiration and pursuit to be like him. He and my brother were solely responsible for having over 35 Congolese children fall deeply in love with Dancehall and other genres of music from the Caribbean. Yann was the first of us boys in my childhood community to go off to boarding school. For some reason this was something to add to one's boasting credentials, and many of us boys who got to visit him at his boarding school would speak about how we would be as cool as him and go to boarding school. To be able to be allowed to be far away from family for a long period of time was unheard of.

But, unlike my brother, there was no personal rapport with Yann. There were occasional threats when I got too big for my moustache - the non-existent one that is. But never a direct relationship within the first decade of us knowing each other.

How time and life can change a lot within and between people. When we met again after our paths had gone different ways, there were hours of conversations filled with memories and nostalgia which laid the foundation for what came years after.

As *From Birthing Waters* began to grow from Crossroads, one long conversation between Yann and I eventually found itself at our dreams. Often, such conversations about dreams end up in vagueness and brief sentences.

"Just seeing how things go."

"Doing my best with all that's going on."

This time around, the combination of nostalgic memory conversations, the challenges and joys of the roles we had as sons, brothers, friends, partners, mentors, work colleagues and many more; the state of personal feelings; and the pressure of goals really unlocked a moment where we really got to speak about the dreams we each had. I shared the growing idea of making *From Birthing Waters* a collection. He had read drafts of different chapters on WhatsApp prior to this conversation, but a lot more came after. In turn, he spoke about Vert Corp, under which Vert Publishing stands—the urge to get off the sidelines and become part of the possibilities for our different communities.

And so Yann said, *"Yes, it is possible."* And he said with his words and immediately followed it with actions that said the same statement.

When I was struggling to bring certain aspects to life, it was his check-in and moments of discussion that fostered enough courage to overcome. At the time, his patience when the dates kept moving back prevented any chance of me retaliating and cancelling any further efforts out of reactionary response. His wise persistence and stubbornness did wonders and held me accountable.

And in the process of witnessing this, Yann gifted me time to also think about my own birthing waters. The one I came from and the ones that may come from me.

Without Yann, there is no Papa Jacques and equally, there would not be this *From Birthing Waters* completed by me and published by Vert Publishing.

HENRI LOPES

Each story in Tribalique is
worth a half-day analysis and
unpacking conversation at the
very least.

I can count the number of African authors I read between the ages of 5 and 16 on one hand. There's much to learn from other writers, and just as equally, there is much to learn from one's own. Unfortunately, marketing and guidance meant that it was easier to pick up a Percy Jackson book as a child than The River Between.

When I did begin to read more African authors, it was authors that wrote in English and they were and remain very relatable. At the same time, there are some things that I understood or saw growing up that were not possible to find in most of the books I had read in English. For example, capturing the patience required to dance a whole Congolese Rumba song.

In 2019, I spent a few months learning French with Mr Diobate in Abidjan. I knew enough French to be able to watch Kirikou and Question Pour un Champion on TV5 with Tate Konda as a child. But the professional le et la never quite clicked, even to this day. Mr Diobate was an amazing teacher who really pushed me in his class, and in an effort to get ahead in class, I went in search of books to read. One of the books, and perhaps my proudest book buys, was Tribalique by Henri Lopes. An old worn book with all its pages. Right on the way to Abidjan Mall from Orca. It wasn't an indoor shop, but a simple mat laid on the ground opposite the petrol station.

Lopes like some of his literary counterparts in the realm of African authors that write in French, mixes a use of matter-of-fact writing with an array of reflective metaphors - whether that is through a former Senegalese soldier in Algeria or two loves that meet among friends with Rumba playing in the background.

A lot is lost in translation so I won't try to communicate what I gained in my comprehension of Tribalique.

The way in which Lopes writes the individual stories stayed in my mind as I wrote *From Birthing Water*. Individual stories that stood on their own but had deep connections to each other in terms of, to me, period, themes, and cultural parallels. He weaves in historical moments into making the backbone of fictional stories that do not entirely feel like fiction by the end of it.

Each story in Tribalique is worth of a half day analysis and unpacking conversation at the very least. It also stood out for me because Lopes is Congolese, but his work makes a mark for Brazza-Congo which is often overlooked because of the size and situation of DRC.

In some ways, I hope that From Birthing Waters speaks to even a speck of Tribalique.

BENJAMIN BABUNGA WATUNA

He brings forward memories
that people may or may not
know about.

In 1965, Kabila le Pere met Che. Years later, as President, he would meet Castro, Fidel. The picture was in a history textbook focused on the Cold War, and the purpose of the photo was to emphasise the validity of the fear of communism spreading. The history class quickly moved back to focus on Castro, the death of Kennedy, and the rising threat of communism.

Kabila, or any other African figure, did not appear again in textbooks or history classes until I started my final years of secondary school. It was valuable to experience centring African figures in history, yet something was always missing—the knowledge of history beyond figures and more into the social fabric. The leadership in Congo has been Kasavubu, Mobutu, Kabila le Pere, Kabila le fils, and Tshisekedi. There are many accounts of how each one rose to power, but they did not do it by themselves. What were people thinking? What was the strategy or lack thereof? What were the propaganda and perspectives of both the majority and minority? And quite simply, why?

For those who grew up and experienced it, these things were not perceived as history but as life. Questions of uncles and aunts would be asked, expecting elaborate answers, and responses would be short. The subconscious assumption is that the facts, decisions, people, and events were already known. For me, they were not.

Oral archives are robust. They can stay alive and be passed on from generation to generation. No books or writings can quite capture the way those memories and stories are told. The challenge with oral archives comes in threefold. First, there is the prioritisation of stories and their relevance. If a carrier of the memories withholds one or never gets the trigger to share the specific memory, then there are limited ways to recover it. Second is the unpredictability of life. What happens when the carrier of the memories passes on? How is the memory retrieved? Third, memory is never exact, and neither is history. If the carrier forgets a name and replaces it with "Ali kwa na rafiki yake." Then, stories and memories tied to that name may not be connected. Regardless, oral memories have survived and can continue to do so with the help of writing to store, remind, and bring attention to memories that should be told.

Benjamin Babunga Watuna is an example of such a writer. He brings forward memories that people may or may not know about. In doing so, he has been able to spur rich conversations and discussions around the events, the causes, and the impact. Through him, I have found questions that bring forth stories that history books in old libraries or expensive archives would have never told me. Here is an example of Babunga Watuna's work:

This tweet was taken directly from Watuna's Twitter feed
on Sunday, February 5, 2023, when it was posted.

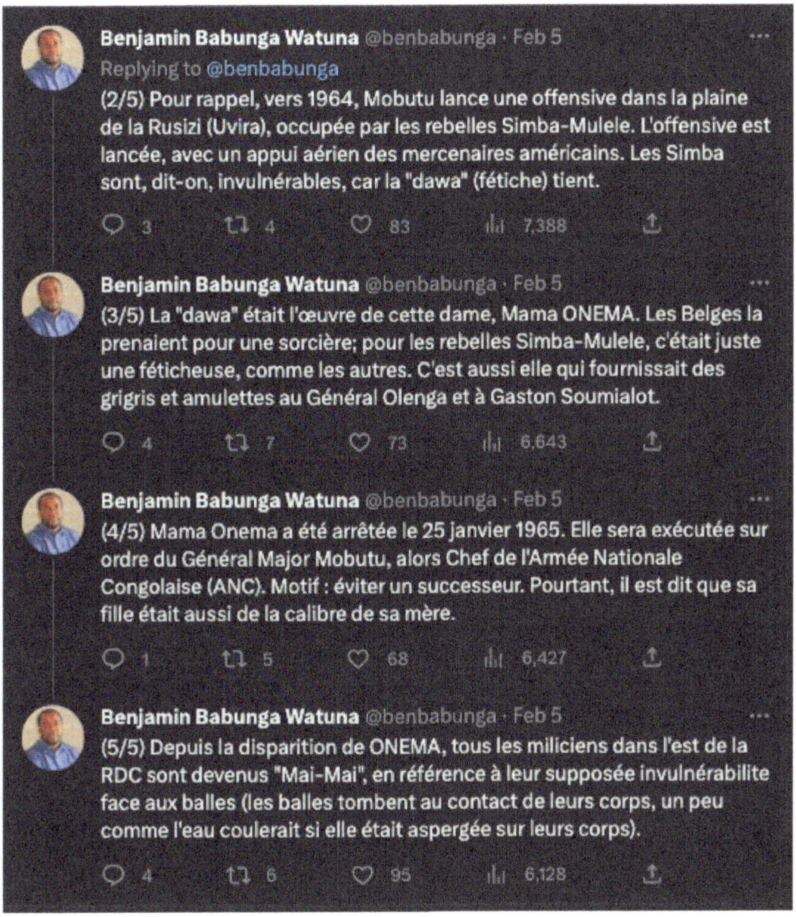

Benjamin Babunga Watuna @benbabunga · Feb 5
Replying to @benbabunga
(2/5) Pour rappel, vers 1964, Mobutu lance une offensive dans la plaine de la Rusizi (Uvira), occupée par les rebelles Simba-Mulele. L'offensive est lancée, avec un appui aérien des mercenaires américains. Les Simba sont, dit-on, invulnérables, car la "dawa" (fétiche) tient.
3 4 83 7,388

Benjamin Babunga Watuna @benbabunga · Feb 5
(3/5) La "dawa" était l'œuvre de cette dame, Mama ONEMA. Les Belges la prenaient pour une sorcière; pour les rebelles Simba-Mulele, c'était juste une féticheuse, comme les autres. C'est aussi elle qui fournissait des grigris et amulettes au Général Olenga et à Gaston Soumialot.
4 7 73 6,643

Benjamin Babunga Watuna @benbabunga · Feb 5
(4/5) Mama Onema a été arrêtée le 25 janvier 1965. Elle sera exécutée sur ordre du Général Major Mobutu, alors Chef de l'Armée Nationale Congolaise (ANC). Motif : éviter un successeur. Pourtant, il est dit que sa fille était aussi de la calibre de sa mère.
1 5 68 6,427

Benjamin Babunga Watuna @benbabunga · Feb 5
(5/5) Depuis la disparition de ONEMA, tous les miliciens dans l'est de la RDC sont devenus "Mai-Mai", en référence à leur supposée invulnérabilite face aux balles (les balles tombent au contact de leurs corps, un peu comme l'eau coulerait si elle était aspergée sur leurs corps).
4 6 95 6,128

This tweet was taken directly from Watuna's Twitter feed on Sunday, February 5, 2023, when it was posted.

At the time, his handle was @benbabunga, as displayed in the photos above. Although this particular thread is unrelated to some of the historical influence weaved into From Birthing Waters, it demonstrates the way in which Babunga brings forward mostly the history, mostly the history that makes the Congolese fabric.

Watuna's thread on Mama Onema explains how she was the spiritual leader of the rebel group Simba-Mulele and reinforced them with spiritual powers. She was captured in January 1965 and forced to be recorded asking Simba-Mulele members to disarm. This came after Mobutu ordered an offensive attack in 1964. Allegedly, Mama Onema's powers and dawa made the members invulnerable. After her execution, members of the group in the east referred to themselves as Mai-Mai, as bullets would slide off them in a similar effect to water. The brief recount of Mama Onema is fascinating in two parts. First, it brings forward a woman's name in a history that often talks solely about the men, not as an empowering women's approach, but simply because women were as much a part of these events as their male counterparts. Second, the connections that are made in Babunga's thread open a door of new questions for someone like me. I grew up hearing about Mai-Mai and the terror that came with them, but there wasn't a thought to ask why they called themselves Mai-Mai. Babunga directly connects one figure's demise to the rise of others.

Two last things must be said about Watuna's work. First, his dedication to sharing and archiving all this history on platforms that are freely accessible by Congolese themselves. Arguably, he could have monetised this into a book that would sit comfortably in libraries of institutions where Congolese people were likely to be the minority in the demographic. Instead, he places these moments in history on Twitter more extensively on his site Babunga Raconte..... babunga.alobi.cd.

The final thing about Babunga is that his thread on Monseigneur Christophe Munizihirwa Mwene Ngabo, whom I briefly speak about next, is what I drew from to tell the story of the assassination of Benjamin Mugabo in From Birthing Waters. If for nothing else, Babunga's dedication should not be forgotten as it teaches and fosters the learning of oneself extensively in a fashion that has evolved with the resources available yet still keeps some of the fundamental roots of how stories and memories are told from where we come from

MONSEIGNEUR MUNZIHIRWA MWENE NGABO

Churches usually have a
picture of an Archbishop and
the Pope at the time, so I
assumed it was the same thing -
honouring role models in
practising religion and faith.

Ever since I was a child, my family had a tradition once we crossed the bridge into Bukavu. Our first stop was in Nguba to greet ba Tate zala Maman - Tate Tina and Tate Konda. Then we would drive through town to Buholo II to see Tate Muzala Papa - Tate M'Chagane before returning to La Mairie to greet Papa JM - Dad's older brother by two. Once all the greetings were done, we would return to our place of stay for our time in Bukavu. What's the connection with Monseigneur Ngabo?

To drive from Nguba to Mairie, La Beaute, or Buholo II, one had to drive past Soko ya Nyawera, right next to Place Munzirihwa. As a child, I used to see his painted frame and assume that he was the epitome of holiness in Bukavu - a predominantly Catholic town. Churches usually have a picture of an Archbishop and the Pope at the time, so I assumed it was the same thing - honouring role models in practising religion and faith. I probably passed the frame at least four times on any given day. And I never really asked much about it. It was there, and many around me didn't bat an eye, so I followed suit.

I first heard of Archeveque's fate in a chance conversation I was sitting through with Papa Gang. There wasn't much more explanation, but it was simply used as a reminder that being holy, religious, or spiritual does not make one immune to the politics of society. I never followed up on it. It wasn't the core of the story being told.

Picture taken from Page 34 of Bukavu | City Gallery on Sky Scraper City started by @BUTEMBO21 https://www.skyscrapercity.com/threads/ bukavu-city-gallery.674930/page-34

Picture taken from Page 34 of Bukavu | City Gallery on Sky Scraper City started by @BUTEMBO21 https://www.skyscrapercity.com/threads/ bukavu-city-gallery.674930/page-34

It was only on October 29th 2022, that I got a Twitter notification about Babunga's post shared below:

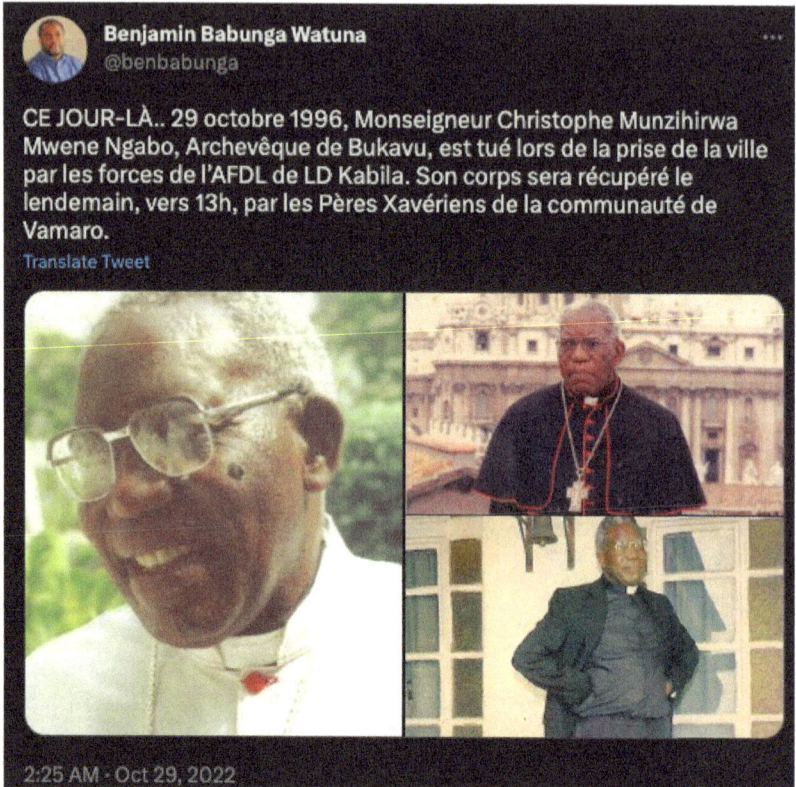

Benjamin Babunga Watuna
@benbabunga

CE JOUR-LÀ.. 29 octobre 1996, Monseigneur Christophe Munzihirwa Mwene Ngabo, Archevêque de Bukavu, est tué lors de la prise de la ville par les forces de l'AFDL de LD Kabila. Son corps sera récupéré le lendemain, vers 13h, par les Pères Xavériens de la communauté de Vamaro.

Translate Tweet

2:25 AM · Oct 29, 2022

On Tuesday, 29th October 1996, Kabila le Pere's military group AFDL took Bukavu by force. The town becomes calm at around 4.30 p.m. after a day of gunshots. Monseigneur Munzihirwa Mwene Ngabo decided to take that opportunity to drive to College Alfajiri, where a group of sisters'/nuns' safety was at risk.

Benjamin Babunga Watuna @benbabunga · Oct 29, 2022 ···
Replying to @benbabunga
(2/6) Ce 29 octobre 1996, Bukavu se réveille avec la peur car des armes lourdes se font entendre, surtout vers Nyangezi. En ville, la tension ne fait que monter et on entend des coups tirés dans chaque point de la ville. Mais vers 16h30, il y a un bref instant de calme.
2 9 47

Benjamin Babunga Watuna @benbabunga · Oct 29, 2022 ···
(3/6) C'est là que Mgr Munzihirwa décide de se diriger vers le collège Alfajiri pour chercher à aider un petit groupe de sœurs, dont la sécurité n'était pas garantie. Il conduit seul sa voiture, accompagné de son chauffeur et d'un agent de la gendarmerie affecté à sa protection.
1 10 46

Benjamin Babunga Watuna @benbabunga · Oct 29, 2022 ···
(4/6) Arrivé à Nyawera (centre-ville), la voiture est forcée à s'arrêter par des coups de feu de quelques militaires. Mgr Munzihirwa descend et se dirige vers les militaires. Après un échange de phrases, les militaires l'obligent à aller, peu distant, vers un poteau électrique.
3 10 43

Benjamin Babunga Watuna @benbabunga · Oct 29, 2022 ···
(5/6) Le gendarme et son chauffeur seront assassinés sur le champ. Ceux qui se trouvaient dans une autre voiture, arrêtée derrière celle de l'archevêque, et qui avaient réussi à prendre la fuite et à se cacher, avaient suivi chaque mouvement.
1 11 43

Benjamin Babunga Watuna @benbabunga · Oct 29, 2022 ···
(6/6) Ils confirmeront que jusqu'à 18h30, Mgr était encore vivant, appuyé sur le poteau électrique, dans une longue discussion au téléphone cellulaire et que c'est en début de soirée que ses bourreaux décideront de l'abattre : des coups à la nuque et Mgr s'affaissa sur le sol.
1 13 44

He drives himself to College but is accompanied by his driver and his allocated protection from the military. As they arrive in Nyawera on their way to College, they are stopped by some militants who fire off a few gunshots. Monseigneur steps down from his car and talks with the men who stopped him, and they let him advance to an electric pole a little further ahead. At this point, they kill his bodyguard and driver instantly. People in the cars behind Monseigneur managed to escape and take shelter. They provide accounts of what transpired through their witnessing of the following events. Still alive, Monseigneur is witnessed on the electric pole talking at length on the cellphone. Until 6.30 p.m. on October 29th 1996, Monseigneur was still alive. It is at this point that the men, his executioners, decide to kill him. Shots are fired. Monseigneur is hit in the neck. Monseigneur collapses to the ground. Dead.

His body remained on the street until 1 p.m. the following day, Wednesday 30th October 1996, when the Xaverian Brothers collected his body. A body that had been on the street for about 18 hours: eighteen hours is 75% of a day.

Photo taken from Jean-Baptiste Malenge's blog PRÊTRE DANS LA RUE Jan 20, 2017, article: POUR LA BÉATIFICATION DE MGR CHRISTOPHE MUNZIHIRWA, L'ARCHEVÊQUE DE BUKAVU A INSTALLÉ UN TRIBUNAL ECCLÉSIASTIQUE (https://pretredanslarue.blogspot.com/2017/01/ pour-la-beatification-de-mgr-christophe.html)

The picture above was taken on January 16, 2017, when the Archdiocese of Bukavu prayed for the opening of a new chapter after Monseigneur Christophe Munzirihwa Mwene Ngabo's beatification.

ABOUT JAMAL "CREATOR" MABULAY

Jamal Mabulay, known professionally as Jamal_Creator, is a Congolese illustrator born in the picturesque town of Goma, where he spent his formative years. A lifelong drawing enthusiast, he embarked on his professional journey in 2010, creating satirical caricatures for the "Jeune Congolais" newspaper and depicting current events on his Instagram page. He holds a law degree from the Protestant University of Congo in Kinshasa and gained further recognition by co-organizing the Manga and Geek Days drawing contest.

Jamal's artistic style is distinctly caricatural and cartoonish, with a preference for unrealistic portrayals, oversized ears, and the "Shibi" style featuring diminutive figures. Classic animations from Disney and Cartoon Network heavily inspire his work. His career includes initial work with "Jeune Congolais," contributions to Manga and Geek Days, and a role as a creative consultant at Effektive Studios.

ABOUT VERT PUBLISHING

Vert Publishing, founded in 2022, is a dynamic company that champions original works and inspires young Africans at home and abroad to explore their creativity through publishing. We are committed to creating a platform where diverse voices can flourish and make a meaningful impact on both individual lives and broader communities.

Under the leadership of Yann, an avid poetry writer and spoken word enthusiast, we specialize in a wide range of content and genres. Our publications, from poetry to captivating fiction and non-fiction, showcase the rich cultural tapestry of Africa and its diaspora. Our inaugural publication, "From Birthing Waters" by Nteranya Ginga, powerfully explores identity and growth, setting the standard for our future offerings.

As a collaborative publisher, we work closely with our talented authors and artists. We provide the necessary guidance and support to refine their work, ensuring that each piece not only resonates deeply with readers but also remains true to the creator's vision. Our goal is to spark conversations, challenge perspectives, and foster renewed creativity and self-expression.

In our next adventures, we will be bringing you :
Siri Yabo
Family Dishonour

ABOUT THE AUTHOR

Nteranya Sanginga, a Congolese creative, excels in a spectrum of artistic endeavours marked by significant collaborations and solo projects. Noteworthy among their contributions is the co-authored piece "What the Atlantic Got Wrong on Congo – A Long Open Letter," alongside Tshimundu, Koko Ginga, and J. Munroe, and their involvement in "Germaine" for Iminza's album "Roots X Wings." They have pushed their creative versatility further through collaborations with artists such as Won Young Mbengeni, David Gyampo, and the Youth Theatre of Kenya.

As a former member of the Afrocontigbo Dance Company, founded by Korma Aguh-Struckmayer, Sanginga's artistic journey is enriched by learning from Patricia Brown, Djenane Saint-Juste and Fofo of Afoutayi Haitian Dance, Arts and Music Company, Leanna Browne, Wynn Fricke, and Karen Charles. Their performances include Afoutayi's "Konesans" (2017 & 2018), Leslie Parker's "crystal, smoke n' spirit(s)" (2019) at the Momentum New Dance Works Festival, and Threads Dance Project's "Tapestries 4.0" (2019).

Made in the USA
Monee, IL
05 September 2024

65192048R00125